For my classmate
- 50 4

Murder by Proxy

by

Suzanne Young

Suzanne Young
Oct. 2013

Mainly Murder Press, LLC

PO Box 290586
Wethersfield, CT 06109-0586
www.mainlymurderpress.com

Mainly Murder Press

Copy Editor: Paula Knudson
Executive Editor: Judith K. Ivie
Cover Designer: Karen Phillips

Mainly Murder Press
www.mainlymurderpress.com

Copyright © 2011 by Suzanne Young
ISBN 978-0-9827952-3-1

Published in the United States of America

2011

Mainly Murder Press
PO Box 290586
Wethersfield, CT 06109-0586

Dedication and Acknowledgments

To Joan (in memory) and Anne Budlong, who took
me in and introduced me to Colorado

My gratitude to Larry Marsh for sharing his ideas and
expertise on automobile mechanics that led to several
possible plot scenarios, including one used in this story.
Heartfelt thanks to Sandi Marsh for her work on the web site
www.SuzanneYoungBooks.com.

For support above and beyond during the release of my
first novel, I cannot express my thanks enough to Carolyn
Knudsen, Anna Lindsey, Kaitlin Lindsey and "Little Alice" of
the Clear Creek Animal Hospital. Their generosity and
kindness to all creatures great and small is exceptional.

I extend my appreciation to the men and women of the
Arvada (Colorado) Police Department, sworn officers and
civilians alike, for their dedication and well-organized,
informative citizens' police academy.

During my brief emergency stay at Lutheran Medical
Center, the following people were incredibly kind and
reassuring: Shelly, admit nurse; Laurie & Heidi, third floor
RNs; Deborah, third floor CAN (nurse assistant); Sandra,
echo cardiology; and "transporter" Lee (also a jolly member
of the Renaissance Festival cast).

I am indebted to my friends Jim Coleman, Olivia Coleman,
Lori Gee and Gail Lindsey for their expertise and feedback as
first readers.

I especially wish to thank and acknowledge my best critics
Linda Berry and Bonnie McCune without whose support and
guidance this story never would have come to life; and Jodie
Ball, our newest writing partner, for her insights and
suggestions.

One

Why would someone run down a young woman and not stop? Edna Davies wondered with an inward shudder as she slid into the rearmost pew of the chapel.

The casket was closed, its lid covered with a spray of flowers surrounding a photograph of the dead woman. Edna guessed it was a college graduation picture. The same photo had been used for the cover of the memorial card that was being handed out at the door. The card looked home grown, a computer-generated four-fold designed by a loving hand.

She hadn't wanted to come to the funeral, let alone go up to the altar, but she had done it for her son who seemed to take strength from having her near. Once Grant laid his single rose on the coffin with the other flowers, he had escorted her to the back pew before joining the other pallbearers. He walked slowly, stiffly, shoulders hunched. She had never seen him look so forlorn, not even at his first wife's funeral.

Waiting for the service to begin, she studied the picture on the card. Lia Martin had been a pretty brunette with long, straight hair. A mischievous twinkle shone in her large, dark eyes, obvious even in the formal photograph. Twenty-four years old, Grant had told Edna. Lia had been jogging at dawn when a dark-colored SUV struck her down. The driver never even slowed, according to the only witness who had come forward.

Edna shook her head in a combination of disbelief and dismay. She looked up to watch her son talking with two other men at the front of the small church. Lia had been Grant's systems administrator, whatever that meant, but Edna gathered it was an important position in his computer department. The company he worked for was a large distributor of office products.

Of her four children, Grant was the only one whose stocky build resembled her side of the family. The other three were all lean and lanky, taking after their father. Grant also had her fair skin, more apt to burn than tan, and auburn hair with a tendency to curl. Although hers had long since gone gray, the curl was still there.

She didn't feel her sixty-eight years at all until the thought occurred to her that she had been Lia's age when she'd given birth to Matthew, her first baby, and that Grant, her third, would be thirty-two in March. As she thought of her offspring, she caught a glimpse of Lia's parents. They were standing by their daughter's coffin, and as Edna looked up, the father bent to kiss his wife's temple. No one should have to bury a child.

"Mrs. Davies?"

Startled out of her reverie, she was momentarily disoriented. Was someone calling her name? She didn't know anybody here. Perhaps she hadn't heard correctly. Moving her head casually, she glanced left, then right, scanning the people around her.

"Excuse me. Mrs. Davies?"

The voice was low and hoarse, scarcely above a whisper. Unexpectedly, a shiver prickled down her spine.

She was about to turn around when a young couple appeared beside her, wanting to share the pew. As Edna slid sideways to make room, her tote bag fell from her lap onto the floor. She bent and fumbled to pick it up, wedging herself between the seat and the back of the neighboring bench as she simultaneously clutched her coat to keep it from following the bag and struggled to keep her wide-brimmed black hat on her head. Feeling flustered and a little breathless, she finally resettled herself and turned to see who had called her name. She saw nobody. Had she imagined it?

"Ladies and gentlemen ..."

Wishing again that she had never agreed to accompany her son to this funeral, Edna focused her attention on the woman who rose to address the gathering. The speaker, whom Edna guessed to be in her early thirties, looked stiffly professional in a black business suit, her blond hair pulled into a bun at the base of her skull. Referring to the card in her hand, Edna noted that the woman was Marcie James, a sales supervisor at Grant's company.

The service progressed while Edna's thoughts wandered again, this time to the house where she and her husband Albert had lived for barely two months, their retirement home in southern Rhode Island. Even with boxes still left to unpack and flower beds to winterize before the first hard frost hit, Albert had talked her into accepting Grant's plea for help.

Last year Albert had sold his share of a successful family medical practice near Providence. Almost at once, he and Edna set off on a driving trip that had taken them along the eastern seaboard, nearly to Florida, in search of the perfect place to live out the rest of their lives.

Eventually, they had returned to their home state, finding nothing as versatile or alluring as the familiar beaches, fields and forests of Rhode Island.

The day they returned home, Albert began receiving calls from former colleagues, asking his opinion on one medical case or another. Most recently, an invitation had been extended for him to speak at a conference in Chicago. From Illinois, he had flown to Colorado to visit a progressive children's clinic, which gave him the opportunity to spend a few days with their son.

During Albert's visit Grant's second wife, Karissa, had been rushed to the emergency room, almost delivering her baby in its seventh month. Her physician, with whom Albert heartily agreed, told the young woman that she should remain in bed for the next two months if she were to carry her baby full term. Actually, she wasn't strictly bedridden. She could get up for meals or to use the bathroom. She could even lie on the sofa in the living room if she wished, but her activities were severely restricted.

It was for this reason that Albert had called Edna, and she had agreed to help. Karissa's own mother had died of cancer five years ago, and there were no other female relatives or friends who could commit to an indeterminate stay. Edna thought she and Albert would handle things together, but she had been in Colorado only two days when Albert, the traitor, had flown back home in answer to a desperate call from another colleague requesting his consultation with a particularly baffling medical case. For a retired physician, he certainly was keeping awfully busy.

Abruptly, her attention was brought back to the present when people around her stood and began filing out of the chapel. She had no more time to dwell on her thoughts as she rode with several other mourners in a minivan to the burial site. Having arranged earlier to meet Grant after the graveside service, Edna hurried to keep up with her fellow passengers after they were dropped off. She was thankful she had worn sensibly low heels but wished for her walking shoes as she traversed the uneven lawn.

Standing slightly apart from the crowd, she watched her son help lift the coffin from the hearse. The sun was harshly bright, and in the early October breeze, leaves chased themselves in a race to the open grave.

"Mrs. Davies?"

She spun around, recognizing the low, hoarse voice as the one she had thought she'd heard in the chapel. A man came up on her right, hat in hand, towering over her in a rumpled brown suit and looking every bit like an oversized bloodhound with his loose jowls and sad brown eyes. His smile was weak, apologetic. "Name's Ernie Freedman. Be obliged if you'd spare a minute when this is over."

"What do you want?" She was baffled. She was two thousand miles from home, and this stranger was talking to her as if he knew her.

"I'd like to tell you a story, Ma'am." He spoke quietly. "Maybe after you hear it …" he paused briefly before continuing. "Well, you see, I'm hoping you'll help me."

"Who are you? How do you know my name?" She became aware her voice had risen when several people turned to look at them. She hadn't realized the graveside prayer had begun.

Not wishing to disturb the mourners further, she turned and took the stranger's arm, leading him a short distance away. She almost never acted on impulse, had always been careful to consider the propriety of a given situation, but at the moment, she was glad for the diversion. The burial of a woman nearly the age of her own youngest child disturbed her more than she had anticipated.

Once they were out of earshot, she stopped and repeated her question. "How do you know who I am?"

He smiled, making his sad eyes twinkle for an instant. "Your son bears quite a resemblance to you. I guessed at the relationship when I saw him escorting you to your seat back at the chapel."

Edna couldn't help smiling herself before becoming serious again. "Who are you?"

"I'm a detective, Ma'am."

"For heaven sakes, stop calling me that. It makes me feel old. My name's Edna." She thought Ernie didn't look much younger than she. Five or six years, perhaps. In his early to mid-sixties, she guessed. No younger. "What do you want from me?"

"It's really your son I'm after. I need to talk to him."

"Then why not do so?"

"He's avoiding me." Ernie toyed with his cloth hat, twisting the brim in his large hands.

Edna was losing patience. She did not feel like playing Twenty Questions with this stranger. "Look, Mr. Freedman, unless you can tell me straight out what it is you want, please go away." She started to turn back toward the gravesite.

"No. Wait. I need you to ask Grant to listen to me." He reached out a hand but didn't touch her. "See, I'm looking for a friend of his. Woman named Anita Collier."

Fumbling in an inside jacket pocket, he pulled out a wallet-sized picture and handed it to her.

Taking the small photo and thinking the name sounded familiar, Edna studied the picture of a young woman with straight, dark hair. Startled and confused, she glanced up at Ernie. "She looks like Lia, the one who's being buried today."

"I know." He indicated the photo in her hand. "Actually, they were friends. Both worked at Office Plus with your son."

"How can Grant help you?"

Hope filled his eyes as Ernie slapped the rumpled hat onto his thinning gray hair. "I'm not real sure. I'd wanted to talk to Lia, but now that she's gone, Grant is the only lead I have left. I know he and Anita are friends. For one thing, he recorded the message on her answering machine."

"Why is that significant? Lots of women ask a male acquaintance to record their phone greetings. There's probably no more to it than that." Not certain whether she was convincing herself or the detective, she said, "He could have done that at the office, if they work together as you say."

"Sure, maybe, but he changed this particular message only yesterday. Oh, the intent was the same, can't come to the phone blah blah blah. But it's been reworded, and he did it sometime yesterday."

"So?" Edna was still confused as to what Freedman was driving at.

He squinted for a moment at the distant mountains with their snow-capped peaks. When he met her eyes again, he spoke slowly, as if trying to get things straight in his own mind as well. "Your son changed a taped message yesterday for a woman who hasn't been seen or heard from for more than a month. It could be some sort of signal or coded message for her, or maybe she asked him to do it. Either way," he paused meaningfully, "he's in contact with her. I'm sure he knows where she is, but for some reason, he doesn't want her found. I'm wondering why."

Two

"Ma?"

Edna turned to see Grant striding toward them. As he drew nearer, she saw the question in his eyes turn to anger. "What are you doing here?" He walked up close to the older man and hissed, "Stop following me." His face was becoming flushed and mottled.

She took hold of her son's arm, hoping to calm him. "Grant? He's only trying to find your friend. What's the matter with you?"

"Please stay out of this." He shook her off gently but firmly. "You don't know anything about it." Grant pointed a finger at the man's face, causing Ernie to step backward. "I told you before, I'm not answering any of your questions." Turning, he grabbed Edna's arm and marched her off toward the parking lot. "Ma, I want you to stay away from that guy."

She didn't like it when he called her "Ma." He did it only when he was upset or worried and that, in turn, upset her. Rarely did Grant show a temper, and it frightened her to realize how distraught he'd become. It was all she could do to keep pace with him. Used to living at sea level, she became breathless when she climbed stairs or walked too fast in this mile-high city.

As they approached Grant's ancient red Toyota Celica, she saw several people gathered near the car. Her son seemed to have his anger in check by the time they reached the group, and he began introductions.

"Ma, this is Marcie James, field sales supervisor at Office Plus. Marcie, my mother, Edna Davies."

Edna recognized the professional-looking woman who had given the first eulogy. Sensitive to people's facial expressions, Edna had the distinct impression she and Grant had interrupted a steamy argument between Marcie and the man Grant introduced next.

"This is Rice Ryan, vice president of marketing for the company."

"A pleasure to meet you, Mrs. Davies." His smile creased his tanned cheeks and crinkled the corners of his blue-gray eyes.

She gazed up at the ruggedly handsome man in his impeccable three-piece suit. With his weathered skin and a nose that had been broken at least once, Rice looked more like a man who should be wearing faded jeans, a Stetson hat and chaps instead of tailored business attire. She was about to take his proffered hand when she realized she still held the picture Ernie had given her. Stuffing it quickly into her tote bag, she shook Rice's hand. "How do you do."

"And this is Brea Tweed, Ma, Rice's secretary."

"Administrative assistant." Brea pouted at Grant. She was a well-endowed young woman with startlingly red hair carefully arranged in a cropped, just-got-out-of-bed look. She batted her eyes at the men around her, swaying her hips and shoulders seductively as if to make the most of their attention before turning to Edna. "So pleased to meet you." She didn't offer to shake hands.

"Sorry, I forgot your name," Grant said, turning to the fourth person in the group.

"Yonny." He shook Grant's hand before turning to Edna. "Yonny Pride. Nice to meet you, Mrs. Davies."

He looked to Edna to be of Slavic descent with his angular frame and high cheekbones. He, too, was good looking but in a dark, brooding way. Unlike Rice, he wore clothes that looked more natural on him, a black leather jacket over casual black slacks. He was half a head taller than either Grant or Rice.

"If you'll excuse us, I have to get my mother back to the house." Grant reached around Marcie to open the Celica's passenger door for Edna.

"We were all just leaving," Rice said, clicking a remote device to unlock the doors of a silver Lexus parked next to Grant's beat-up Toyota. Marcie and Brea moved to the passenger side of the Lexus as Rice turned to Grant who was rounding the back of his own car.

Grant had left the windows partially opened. Although the air temperature outside was cool and crisp, the interior of the car was as hot as an oven from the intense Colorado sun. As she rolled her window down completely, Edna heard a harsh whisper, "Where is she?" and looked in the side mirror in time to see Grant shake off Rice's grip on his wrist.

"Supposing that I did know, you'd be the last person I'd tell," was Grant's hissed reply.

Glancing around, Edna was certain she was the only witness to this exchange.

"I'm still married to her. I have legal rights, so you'd better tell me where she is."

Edna looked again into the side mirror in time to see Rice's hand squeeze into a fist. Certain he was going to lash out at her son, she reached to open her door but was stopped by movement inside the neighboring car. Marcie had leaned over from the passenger's seat and was pushing open the driver's door. "Come on, Rice. Let's go. We're cooking in here."

The two men stood glaring at each other for a few seconds longer, as if neither wanted to be the first to look away. At Marcie's angry, "Rice, what's holding you up?" he turned and slipped into the driver's seat, slamming the door.

Edna turned, waiting for Grant to open the driver's door of the Celica. She wanted to ask him about the angry display, but the sound of Rice's tires squealing on asphalt made her spin around as the Lexus peeled out of the parking lot. Twisting to look after the Lexus, she noticed Yonny, several spaces away, folding himself into a white, two-door Ford Escort. Momentarily distracted by the sight, she was wondering why he didn't have a bigger car for his long legs, when Grant slipped into the seat beside her. His dour mood had returned as he drove out of the parking lot and turned the car toward home.

"What was Rice so angry about?" she said, hoping to get Grant to open up to her and let off some steam in the process.

"Nothing," Grant muttered, keeping his eyes on the road.

She prodded her son with a comment. "You all work together, I take it."

"All but that guy Yonny. I only met him recently. He's … he was one of Lia's rock-climbing friends."

Mention of the dead woman made Edna remember what Ernie had said. "Who is Anita Collier? That man at the cemetery said she was also a friend of Lia's." *And of yours,* she added mentally, not wanting to risk Grant's further anger by speaking that thought aloud.

Grant scowled at the road ahead and let out a deep breath before answering. "Yes, she was a friend, and before you ask, I don't know why she wasn't at the funeral."

Since her son finally seemed resigned to her probing, Edna was determined to find out as much as she could. "And Anita is a friend of yours, too?"

He glanced at her for an instant. "Why do you want to know about her?"

She shrugged. "It's just that her name seems familiar. Who is she?"

Grant didn't say anything for such a long time, Edna began to wonder if he were going to answer at all. "She was Michele's best friend." He paused briefly before continuing. "Remember how reluctant Michele was to move out here, away from our families?"

"Yes." The pain that hit her chest at the mention of Grant's first wife, dead less than a year, kept Edna from saying more. She took several slow breaths before she could manage a weak smile in her son's direction. "It didn't take her long to adjust, though, once you got settled here."

"No," he agreed. "That was thanks to Anita."

"Oh?" She encouraged him to go on.

"When I took the job at Office Plus five years ago, Anita was Rice's secretary."

"Administrative assistant." Trying to allay some of her own melancholy, Edna pouted, imitating Brea, and was rewarded in her attempt at humor by a snort from her son.

"Yes, well ... whatever." Grant chuckled again,

shaking his head before going on. "Rice was head of operations, which included the computer department, so at that time my boss reported to him. I was just another new employee in a growing company, but Anita was nice enough to stop by my desk once in a while and ask how things were going. One day, we happened to meet in the coffee room. I don't know how it began, but I started telling her about how unhappy my wife was. Because of it, I was having trouble concentrating on things at the office. I thought maybe I was going to lose my job."

"I think that's what Michele wanted to happen," Edna interjected, thinking back to telephone conversations with her daughter-in-law. Actually, she, too, had been secretly hoping Grant would move his family back to Providence. She had particularly missed her precocious three-year-old granddaughter, but then Michele's attitude began to change. Grant's next words brought Edna's attention back to his story.

"Anita must have called Michele as soon as she got back to her desk that morning. They hadn't even met, but Anita introduced herself and invited Michele to lunch, said definitely the invitation included Jillian, so a babysitter wouldn't be necessary." Grant grinned at his mother before turning his eyes back to the road. "She took them to the cafeteria at the Museum of Natural History. Museum of Nature and Science, I guess they call it now. Anyway, the three of them had a blast. Jillybean went nuts over the giant tyrannosaurus rex. Michele told me that Jillian sat for the longest time and just stared up at all those bones while Anita told her about dinosaurs. Lunch was such a success that Anita called in to take the rest of the afternoon off, and that day was the beginning of Michele's turnaround. Anita toured her all over Denver, introduced her to people, and had her signing up for aerobics classes, museum trips and outdoor concerts. She kept Michele and Jillian so busy I was able to get on with my work, and everything was great. Anita became part of our family."

"Is she married? Does she have children of her own?"

"She and Rice were married a couple of years ago." His frown returned and his grip seemed to tighten on the steering wheel.

So that's who Rice was asking about, she thought, remembering the near altercation in the parking lot.

"It was weird," Grant said. "Rice dated lots of women, and Anita's a real knockout, so I would have thought he'd hit on her right away, but he didn't seem interested other than the fact that she worked for him. At the time, I figured he thought she was too young. I don't know what sparked him, and I don't think Anita really did either, but one day it was like he became obsessed with her. He kept asking her out and buying her flowers and gifts. She resisted for a long time, not only because he was her boss but also because he had a reputation for always being out with someone new and never sticking with any one woman for very long. Rice is a guy who likes the chase and gets bored quickly when it's over."

Grant seemed to realize he was gripping the steering wheel too tightly because for a minute he sat back against the seat and flexed the fingers of each hand. When he continued, he spoke as if relating memories, talking to himself as much as to Edna. "Rice really poured on the charm, and Anita finally agreed to have dinner with him, but only after she'd become a field sales rep and Brea had been hired to replace her in the office. By that time, Rice had been promoted to vice president of marketing and sales, so the changes in his staff were logical.

"They hadn't dated for very long when one Friday night, Anita called Michele to say she and Rice were on their way to Las Vegas to get married. Michele tried to talk sense into her, but Anita said she knew what she was doing, and neither she nor Rice wanted the fuss and bother of a big wedding."

"From what I heard back in the parking lot, it sounds like the marriage isn't going well."

"I could have told her it wouldn't last."

"Do they have children?" Grant hadn't answered her question earlier, and she hoped there weren't children involved. It was bad enough when couples split up, but she didn't like thinking how it affected their young ones.

"No. Rice didn't want kids. I think that's what made her finally wake up and see him for what he really is, a good-time guy with no sense of responsibility. Anita has always wanted a big family. She's an only child and says she regrets not having brothers or sisters. She and Michele were always arguing the pros and cons of single child versus siblings. Since Michele had three sisters, she thought being an only child would have been wonderful." Grant turned to smile again at his mother. "I took Anita's side. I don't want Jillybean to miss out on the fun of having a brother or sister."

It looks like you're getting your wish, Edna thought, picturing Grant's second wife, home in bed for the remaining weeks of her pregnancy. Aloud, she said "Am I guessing correctly that Anita is definitely leaving Rice and has taken back her maiden name?"

"You're half right." Grant concentrated on a right-hand

turn before offering further explanation. "Anita kept her maiden name, never went by Anita Ryan. Probably a good thing because, yes, she's left him. As I mentioned before, Rice never wanted a family. Guess he forgot to tell her that before they got married." His voice dripped with sarcasm. "The honeymoon didn't last long either. Last year, Rice changed Anita's sales territory from metro Denver to a region covering northern Colorado, Wyoming, Montana and northern Idaho. That means she's gone a lot. Very convenient for him, her being out of town, assigned to our most desolate territory."

"What did she have to say about that? Didn't she object?"

"Object? No." Grant glanced at his mother with a grimace. "According to Michele, Rice told Anita it would be good experience for her, give her the challenge she needed to improve her skills. She, in turn, was going to show him what she could do, and she has. That territory was one of the worst for sales, and she's been bringing it around. The latest figures show the region's numbers are up twenty-seven percent over last year.

"Rice was very attentive toward Anita during the few days each month she spent in town. Apparently, everyone but she knew he wasn't being faithful. At least, she didn't say anything to us about it, if she did suspect. Maybe she had her doubts but didn't want to believe the worst of her husband. She was always defending him, no matter what."

"She sounds like someone who doesn't give up easily," Edna observed. "Maybe she felt she could turn her husband around, like she did with her sales territory."

Grant snorted. "You're right about her being a fighter, but Rice can be a real bastard. Sorry, Mother, but there's no nicer word for him. Anita left him a couple months ago, and I was glad to help her move out."

"And he doesn't know where she is." It was more a statement than a question she posed to her son.

He frowned for a moment before his face cleared with understanding. "You heard the disagreement." When she nodded, he turned his eyes back to the road and said, "I'm not so sure that wasn't one of Rice's acts. I think he knows exactly where she is. If he doesn't, he has enough money to put a detective on her trail."

"Do you know where she is?" His mention of a detective brought Ernie's face to her mind, but she was smart enough not to wonder aloud if the man she'd just met might indeed be working for Anita's estranged husband.

He was silent for several minutes before replying. "No, I don't, but I've been hoping to hear from her. With Dad visiting last week and Karissa getting sick, and all the extra work I have preparing for a big software conversion at the office, I haven't had a lot of extra time even to think about looking for her. Since Lia's fatal accident was all over the news, I thought for sure she'd be at the funeral. But she hasn't called, and now that she didn't show up today when one of her best friends was being buried, I'm really starting to worry."

"What made you change her telephone recording? That detective told me you rerecorded it yesterday. He thinks she asked you to do it."

Grant looked surprised. "Is that what he said?" After a brief pause, he explained matter-of-factly. "I did change it, but not because she told me to. She was very particular about her message when I first recorded it. She wrote it down and had me read it exactly. I thought if she were monitoring her phone, she'd call to find out why I changed it. It's a reach, I admit, but it's the only thing I could think of and the only thing I have time for right now."

He took a hand from the wheel and ran it through his close-cropped curls in a gesture of frustration. "It isn't like her not to have called us before this. I would have thought she would at least want to talk to Jillian. She's like a favorite aunt to Jillybean." He paused for a heartbeat before adding with a tone of equal distress, "Even if I had the time, I wouldn't know where to begin to look for her."

Edna considered for a minute before asking, "If you're as anxious to contact her as you say, why won't you talk to that detective? Why won't you let him help you find her?"

They had reached his house, and before answering, he turned into the driveway, parked and shut off the ignition. Facing her, he said, "Because I don't know this guy from Adam. Why is he looking for Anita? For all I know, he's working for Rice." He pushed open the car door, adding, "And whatever her reason, Anita doesn't want to be found."

Three

Edna slid out of the car and rushed after Grant to the front door of his ranch-style, brick house. "What do you mean she doesn't want to be found? Why not? Are you saying that only because you haven't heard from her or because she told you not to look for her?"

He glanced at his watch before opening the door with his key. "I don't have time to discuss it now, Mother. I'm going in to check on Karissa and then I have to get back to work. Please. Stay out of this. I don't want to have to worry about you, too."

Before she could answer he had opened the door, ushered her in, and disappeared down the hall to the master bedroom. Taking her time, she removed her hat, hung up her coat in the small closet to the left of the front door, and looked in a nearby mirror to fluff her gray curls. She was running out of excuses to loiter in the entryway when Grant strode purposely down the hall and through the living room toward her.

"Grant, just a minute."

"I'm late. Mother, I've really got to get back to work." Gently, but firmly, he took her by the shoulders and moved her to one side so he could open the front door. Before he released her, however, he looked straight into her eyes. "Please don't mention any of this to Karissa. She's asleep, so I didn't wake her. You know she's not to be upset. I've been telling her the reason Anita hasn't called is because she wants to be completely alone for a while."

"But ..." was all Edna had time to say before the door closed behind him.

Still depressed over the funeral and newly frustrated at not being able to discover more about the mysterious Anita, Edna went to her small bedroom to change out of her dress into more comfortable slacks and blouse. Returning to the living room, she sat on the cushiony sofa, facing wide French doors that opened onto a redwood deck, and stared out at the backyard.

What was she going to do with herself all day? The weekly cleaners had been in yesterday, and there wasn't enough laundry yet for another load. Jillian wouldn't be home from school until three this afternoon, and it was barely eleven, a good hour before time to make Karissa's lunch. Leaning forward to grab a magazine off the thick wooden coffee table, Edna glanced to her right and down the hall. She would look in on Karissa, but Grant had said she was asleep. Edna didn't feel entirely comfortable with this daughter-in-law yet. She missed Michele and felt that Karissa could never take her place. What was Grant thinking of, marrying so soon after Michele's fatal accident? How could he? Edna leaned back and flipped through the magazine, seeing neither words nor pictures.

If only Albert had stayed to keep her company. At least they would have been able to play cards and keep each other entertained until Jillian came home from school. Right about now they would have been walking around the neighborhood, looking at and discussing various landscaping ideas for their own new home. But Albert had seemed almost relieved when his colleague had called and asked him to consult on the case. He had made the decision to return to Rhode Island instead of trying to advise long distance. "I'm useless around here," he had said. "You'll be fine. I'll call you."

Resenting her husband's desertion, Edna wondered if she shouldn't put her coat on again and take a walk before lunch, but the idea of trudging along the same sidewalks without Albert didn't appeal to her. Tossing the magazine back onto the coffee table, she rose and strolled around the couch. She trailed one hand along the corded fabric on the back of the sofa and studied the room. The furnishings, overstuffed and blockish with little wood showing, were not what she was used to. Definitely not the delicately carved pine and maple antiques that Michele had preferred, but perhaps more practical for a family with young children. Edna had to admit the colors were warm and inviting with a definite western flare in the desert beige, sandstone red and deep sky blue. A large woven basket beside the flagstone fireplace held discarded newspapers. Several small cactus dish gardens set out on side tables complimented the Native American paintings and pottery.

A comfortable, lived-in room, Edna thought, at the same time wondering what had happened to all of Michele's prized possessions she had been so insistent on bringing with her from New England. It must have been expensive to replace an entire houseful of furniture. Michele's pieces had been perfectly serviceable.

She let her mind fill with memories of her late daughter-in-law. Edna had been surprised at Grant's choice in women when she'd first met Michele. The young couple had been undergraduates together at Boston

University, where he was studying computer science and she was an art history major. Michele had been as exuberant as Grant was quiet. Edna, conceding that sometimes opposites attract, welcomed Michele with open arms. She seemed good for Grant, interesting him in parties, dinners and concerts he ordinarily would have shunned. Edna thought back to the elaborate wedding at Michele's family's mansion in East Providence and the huge celebration nearly a year later when Jillian was born.

Since Michele seemed to be the driving force in the marriage, Edna had been amazed when Grant announced their move to Colorado, a decision Michele had opposed vehemently. But he had been enthusiastic about the job opportunity in Denver and relocated his family to the western city five years ago. Although missing them very much and hoping the move was only temporary, Edna had been glad to hear Michele eventually talk animatedly about her new surroundings.

And now she was gone, killed in a skiing accident early last December. Only ten months ago, and Grant had married Karissa in late January, barely two months after Michele's funeral. Except for his younger sister Starling, who had flown out for the ceremony, he hadn't even informed his family until it was over.

How could he have been so disloyal to his first wife? Where had he met Karissa? Were they having an affair while Michele was still alive? There were too many questions for which Edna feared the answers, and she wouldn't pry into her son's private affairs, not until she found a way to do so diplomatically, that is. She had tried getting Starling to talk to her, but all her daughter would say was, "Why don't you ask Grant?"

Starling and Grant were the closest of Edna's four children, in friendship as well as in age. Mathew had been twelve, Diane eight, and Grant fourteen months when Starling was born. It had been like having a second family when the last two came along and they had been almost inseparable growing up. Starling and Michele had become best friends, but what puzzled Edna was that Starling seemed to get along with Karissa just as well. Grant's sister flew to Colorado at least twice a year to visit and vacation. Edna would have been worried that her youngest child would move to Denver, too, except that Starling had a real love affair going with the city of Boston where she was part owner of a photography studio.

And what about Jillybean? Edna smiled, feeling cheered and warm inside thinking of her granddaughter, now eight years old. The family's pet name always made her think of a Mexican jumping bean, an apt description for the energetic youngster. She had inherited her father's looks and her mother's personality.

Karissa, on the other hand, was quiet, like Grant. She smiled a lot and seemed very pleasant, but she wasn't an open book like Michele had been. *It would take a while to get to know her*, Edna thought with a sigh.

She had been walking around the living room with her thoughts, and as she passed the large-paned window that looked out to the front of the house, a motion caught her eye. Moving to the gauze curtains, she pushed one aside an inch or two so she could peer out at the person coming up the walk. *What in the world was he doing here?*

Hurrying to the door, she pulled it open before he could ring the bell and wake Karissa. She stepped out onto the narrow cement stoop and frowned up at the big man.

"Grant isn't here. He's already gone back to work."

"I didn't finish talking to you," Ernie Freedman said with his sad smile, removing his hat.

"My son says I shouldn't speak to you." But despite what Grant had said, she found herself liking this man in the rumpled suit and crumpled tweed hat. Trying not to show her feelings, however, she said, "I'm still not certain who you are or what you want with me."

Wringing the cloth hat in his hands with what she was beginning to recognize as a nervous gesture, he said, "Look, Mrs. Davies. Edna. I've already told you. I'm looking for Anita Collier. I need to find her soon, or she'll lose an enormous fortune. Besides that, her great-aunt will die without any family around. Please, just give me ten minutes."

A sudden gust of wind blew the door inward and chilled Edna in her lightweight blouse. She hesitated for a moment, studying his face. Thinking of how bored she had been just minutes before, she made up her mind. *What's the harm in listening to what he had to say?*

"All right. Come inside. I'll heat some coffee. You can tell me your story. That's what you said at the cemetery, isn't it? That you had a story to tell me."

Ernie's face brightened as he slapped his hat back onto his head. Taking a step forward, he quickly removed it again and stuffed it into a pocket of his suit coat. "Yes, Ma'am, uh, Edna Ma'am."

She almost laughed aloud at his excitement but instead put a finger to her lips. "Shh. Quietly, please. My daughter-in-law is resting. We mustn't disturb her."

Quickly, she preceded him across the living room and through the narrow archway that led to a dining area and kitchen, at the opposite end of the house from the bedrooms. A broad counter separated the two sections of the room, and she indicated he should sit on one of the swivel stools at the bar while she poured what remained of the morning's coffee into two mugs and set them in the microwave.

"At the cemetery you told me you are a detective," she said, waiting for the coffee to heat. She thought of the police officer back home whom she had met recently and who seemed very interested in dating her daughter, another reason for Starling to stay in New England. Aloud, she said, "Are you with the Denver police?"

"No, Ma'am, uh, Edna. I'm private."

"Private? You mean like James Garner in the Rockford Files?" She mentioned one of her favorite old television shows.

Ernie smiled. "Well, yes and no."

"What does that mean, 'yes and no'?"

Ernie brushed a hand over his face and paused for several seconds before replying. "Well for one thing, I don't carry a gun. That's something people always think when you tell them you're a private detective, that you carry a gun. I don't."

"I'm very glad to hear it."

"And I don't go following people around or peeking in their windows, taking pictures. I don't go after people. Things can get messy when a case is about divorce or missing kids or stuff like that."

"I'm happy to hear you're not a Peeping Tom, but if you don't do any of those things, what do you do?" She smiled, trying to put him at ease.

He looked to his right for a minute, staring at the

backyard through the sliding glass door before glancing back at her. He now seemed intent, watching her as if to study her reaction at his next words. "Usually, I find things for people."

"Oh?" She was surprised at his answer. "What sorts of things?"

"Rare coins, stamps, family papers like birth or marriage certificates. Whatever someone wants found."

"I thought people looked for things like that on the Internet these days."

"Yes, well, computers certainly have changed my job. Most of my work lately seems to be hunting down stolen property. Sometimes the local police give my name to burglary victims, and I go hunting for Aunt Maggie's pearl necklace or Mother's wedding ring. I mostly get clients who want me to find sentimental stuff that's been stolen from them."

"Are you successful?" Realizing he might think she was asking if he were wealthy, Edna felt her face grow hot and quickly amended her question. "I mean, do you usually find your client's property?"

"Generally," he nodded, apparently oblivious of Edna's social gaffe, and accepted the coffee mug she handed to him. "I find 'em more often than not."

She came around the counter and perched on a stool beside him, her back to the patio door. She had learned from watching television that it gave someone an advantage if they sat with their back to a window or door, making their facial expressions unreadable in the shadows while the light enhanced the other person's features. Since she had helped to capture a murderer recently, Edna paid more attention to these small details in crime and detective shows. Not that it made much difference in this brightly lighted kitchen, but it certainly didn't hurt to get in some practice.

Thinking of her recent experience in Rhode Island, she said, "I got myself into a situation some weeks ago where I learned more about detecting than I'd ever imagined I would." Then, regretting the momentary lapse into her personal affairs, she immediately turned the conversation back to him. "You say you don't get involved with cases having to do with people, so why are you trying to find this young woman?"

He looked at her sheepishly. "One of my steadiest clients is a lawyer back in New York. Long story how we met, but he sends business my way whenever he can. He knows the sort of work I do, but Monday he calls and asks me to locate this guy, Harrington Collier. Begs me to do this as a special favor to him, just this once, he says. Tells me the guy lives here in Denver, but my client can't get him to return his calls. Says he's been trying to reach Collier for about a week, and it's urgent he get hold of him, and could I just go out to the house and see what's what."

"Collier? A relative of Anita's, I assume?"

"Her father." Ernie took a long swallow of coffee. "Anyway, to get back to my story, I go to the house and nobody's home. House looks deserted, like nobody's been there for a while."

"Are they on vacation?" Edna liked this detective stuff. It wasn't so hard, once you got the hang of it.

"That's what I thought at first, but when I checked with one of the next door neighbors, she told me the Colliers were both killed in a car accident six weeks ago."

"What!" The news was so unexpected that her exclamation was more of a gasp than a question.

"Anita's parents, Harrington and his wife. That's why he hasn't returned my client's phone calls and why I'm now looking for their daughter."

Edna didn't comment on this last remark. She was wondering why Grant hadn't told her about this tragedy in Anita's life. That could explain why she wanted to be alone for a while. "How awful," was all she said aloud.

"About five weeks ago was the last time anyone saw Anita, from what I've been able to find out, about the time of her parents' funeral. I think your son might have seen her since, but I can't get him to tell me anything."

"Edna?" Karissa's voice sounded from the hallway at the other side of the living room.

Edna's heart leaped to her throat. "I'm here, Karissa," she called, sliding off the kitchen stool. Her tone came out in a higher pitch than usual. "Quick," she hissed, pulling at Ernie's arm. "She mustn't see you. Grant will have my hide for letting you in the house." She pushed the glass door open and tugged him out onto the wide, redwood deck. Pointing to the stairs at the far left, she told him to go around the corner and out through the latched gate in the fence.

"I haven't finished," he protested. "Can I come back later?"

"I don't know. I need to make lunch for my daughter-in-law now." Edna was beginning to panic, expecting Karissa to walk through the archway from the living room at any second.

"Please, we gotta talk." He paused for a second or two, before his face brightened. "There's a Safeway not far from here. They have a couple of tables near the deli. Will you meet me there? Please?" He was whispering, pleading as Edna pushed him toward the steps. "It's very important. You gotta hear me out."

"Okay, okay. I'll meet you there in an hour. Now, go!" She gave his shoulder a final push before hurriedly returning to the kitchen, relieved to see Karissa had not yet come into the room. Grabbing Ernie's mug, she rounded the counter, pulled open the dishwasher and upended the cup onto the top rack, sloshing what remained of the coffee over the dishes.

"Edna? Is everything all right? Who are you talking to?" Karissa's voice seemed nearer, but she hadn't yet appeared in the archway.

Edna switched on the small TV set at the end of counter before advancing into the next room. "The television must have been louder than I thought. I'm sorry. Did I wake you?"

"No. The baby did. Guess he or she thought I should get up for lunch. It's about that time, isn't it? I'm not rushing you, am I?" Karissa was sitting on the broad arm of the sofa as if she had stopped to rest before proceeding to the kitchen. From where she sat, she could look through the doorway to the laundry area beyond the kitchen, but neither the counter nor stools were visible.

"You're not rushing me." Edna wished her heart would slow down. She sounded breathless, even to herself. "I must have lost track of the time. Here, let me help you." She moved to Karissa's side to lend her an arm. The petite woman looked like she would topple forward, so heavy was she with the child inside her.

As Edna put a hand beneath her daughter-in-law's

elbow to help her rise, she glanced toward the glass French doors, twins to those leading from the dining room onto the back porch, and saw most of the deck leading to the stairs and down to the backyard. If Karissa had been sitting there when she first called out to Edna, she couldn't have missed seeing Ernie leave.

Four

Over lunch Edna kept up a steady stream of idle chatter, all the while wondering if Karissa had watched Ernie scurry along the back deck or if she had still been in the hallway to the bedrooms when she'd first called to Edna.

"What was Grant like as a little boy?" Karissa had finished her cup of tomato soup and half of a tuna fish sandwich and was sitting back, holding a glass of water in both hands.

Preoccupied with her guilty secret and trying to decide whether or not to bring up the subject of the visitor herself, Edna was taken aback by the question. She took a slow sip of tea to allow herself time to rearrange her thoughts. It wasn't hard to turn back the clock in her head, to hear her children's shouts and laughter. Her mind focused in on her third-born child, and she watched a mental video of Grant, age five, running along the beach at Sand Hill Cove, squealing with delight as he tried to outrun the waves that were swirling up onto the shore to grab at his small ankles.

"He was a happy child. He adored Starling, of course, thought of himself as her protector almost from the day we brought her home from the hospital. He was only fourteen months old himself, but he acted like an old mother hen when it came to his baby sister."

"Has he always hidden his feelings?" Karissa's worried look turned almost instantly to one of apology, as if she were afraid Edna might think she was criticizing Grant. "I mean, that is, he never talks about what's bothering him. Has he always been like that?"

Remembering back, Edna's thoughts stopped at something she hadn't considered in years. "No," she said hesitantly. "He definitely wasn't quiet as a young boy." Pausing, she went over the incident in her mind before explaining aloud. "I had an emergency operation when Grant was ten. Put me in the hospital for almost two weeks and bedridden at home for another six before I was able to get up and move around much. One day, after I'd been in the hospital about ten days, Albert brought the two younger children to visit me. The kids weren't supposed to be there. At that time hospitals worried about children passing colds and such to patients. But I was in a private room, so Albert snuck them up the back stairs. I think, since he was on staff, the nurses turned a blind eye to his breaking the rules that once."

She lowered her cup to its saucer and set them on the table, speaking slowly as the memory rolled through her head. "Mathew was away at college, and Diane was a senior in high school, so it wasn't as much of a mystery for them, but I think my little ones were scared. That's primarily why Albert brought them to see me, to assure them I was okay."

She smiled at Karissa, who was listening intently. "Albert tried to hurry them into the room so nobody would spot them in the hall, but Grant held back, trying to keep a tight grip on Starling's hand. As soon as she saw me, though, she pulled away and ran over to jump up on the bed, but Grant still hung back. When he finally came to my bedside, he laid his head on the pillow next to mine and just stared. I don't know what he was expecting me to do or say, but he stayed like that for quite a long time. Perhaps he imagined I was dying, or maybe he thought he'd never see me again. I think that's when he changed, became quieter. By the time I came home from the hospital, he seemed so much more grown up, very serious and more introspective. During the time I was bedridden, he took care of me as if I were the child and he the adult." She smiled, but the memories brought tears to her eyes. Embarrassed, she fumbled in the pocket of her slacks and pulled out a tissue to wipe her eyes.

"Thank you for telling me." Karissa extended a hand over the table, as far as her enlarged belly would allow.

Edna acknowledged the gesture by reaching out and gently squeezing her daughter-in-law's fingers. Clearing her throat, she said, "I didn't tell you very much."

"Everything I hear puts another piece of the puzzle into place." Karissa smiled and hesitated. "I don't speak my thoughts very clearly sometimes. I hope you know what I mean. I want so much to understand him." It was her turn to look embarrassed. "I should get back to bed." She placed her hands on the arms of her chair and struggled to push herself up.

Edna rushed around the table to help her. Still feeling the sting of unshed tears in her eyes, she said, "I'll think of more cheerful stories for later." As she assisted Karissa down the hall, Edna caught sight of the clock on the mantle and saw it was almost time to meet Ernie. It would take her about fifteen minutes to walk to the grocery store, if she hurried. She would be late, but she had enjoyed lunch and was sorry it was over so soon.

"Karissa, will you be all right by yourself for a little

while?"

Her daughter-in-law laughed. "Of course, Edna. I'm not quite the helpless invalid Grant makes me out to be. I'll be fine. Are you going for a walk?"

Edna felt both guilty and relieved that Karissa made it easy for her to get out of the house. "Yes, I thought I would."

"I don't blame you. It looks like a beautiful day. I wish I could go with you." The young woman smiled wistfully.

"I do too, dear." Edna surprised herself by meaning it. She added quickly. "I'll have my cell phone, and I won't go far, so if you need me, just speed dial my number. Okay?"

The mother-to-be lowered herself onto the bed and promised to call if she needed anything.

Leaving the lunch dishes for later, Edna grabbed her coat and a wide-brimmed straw hat from the closet near the front door. Her skin burned so easily, she couldn't go out into the sun without protecting her head and face. Picking up her tote bag, she stepped outside, stopping on the front walk to button her coat and remind herself of the direction she needed to take.

Edna liked her son's choice of neighborhood. It was an older section of Arvada, a suburb northwest of Denver, with mature trees towering over one-story, single-family dwellings. Several of the lots had lilac bushes or hedges along the property lines, but there were no fences in front. Only the back yards were enclosed and most of those by low chain links. A few yards had higher, wooden privacy fences, but these were mainly homes with swimming pools. Residents in the area seemed to be either young families or elderly, retired couples.

As she looked around, she spotted a shiny black car half a block away. In this neighborhood of minivans and four-wheel-drive vehicles, it was unusual to see a new or sporty car, let alone have it parked on the street. Residents usually garaged their cars or pulled into the driveways. The rear and side windows of this one were darkly tinted, so she couldn't see if anyone was in it. Probably visiting. She shrugged, raised her coat collar against a wind which had picked up and become cooler, and with one hand holding down her hat, headed off in the opposite direction.

Not liking to be late even for an informal appointment such as this one, she hurried toward the neighborhood shopping mall, thinking with some annoyance of Albert returning the rental car to the airport when he'd left. She had wanted to keep the car, but he had decided she wouldn't need it. He reasoned that Grant would do the grocery shopping. Besides, Edna didn't know the city and was no longer used to heavy traffic and highway driving, since Albert chauffeured them whenever they went out.

"What if there's an emergency?" she had asked.

"Dial 911," Albert responded.

"Or call me on my cell phone and I'll come home. I'm only a half hour away," Grant interjected.

She knew her son wanted to be helpful, but he hadn't aided her cause with that suggestion.

"Besides, Sweetheart, I'd worry about you if I thought you were driving around this big city by yourself." Albert had ended the discussion and hugged her warmly before leaving to catch his plane.

She thought of the navy blue 4-Runner Grant had driven to work last week. Since Monday it had been sitting in the garage under a dust cover. Maybe she would ask

him if he would lend her the Celica, and he could use the
SUV. She didn't relish the thought of driving around a
strange city in a large, unfamiliar car, but she could
manage fine in the smaller one.

She could always get another rental using her credit
card, if Grant didn't like the idea of her using his car. *I'm
surprised Albert left me alone to care for Karissa and Jillian if he
feels I'm that helpless*, she thought, beginning to fume, not
for the first time since Albert's hurried departure.

Aware of her growing agitation, she forced her mind
off the subject and concentrated on her meeting with Ernie.
She didn't know if she would, or even could, be of help to
him, but she was intrigued with his story and wanted to
hear more. Who was this Anita Collier? Edna mentally
reviewed some of what she had learned so far. As her
thoughts sorted out the information, she began to feel
queasy. Anita had been a friend of Michele, and now
Michele was dead. Apparently, so were Anita's parents
and another of her friends, Lia Martin. Thinking of the
mystery novels she'd read and crime stories she'd watched
on television, Edna reminded herself that in those stories
characters were always saying there was no such thing as a
coincidence. Could all these fatal accidents somehow be
connected? If they were, Anita was certainly a link.

She felt her unease grow. What about Anita herself? Is
she another victim? If she's alive, why hasn't anyone seen
or heard from her?

As she carefully traversed the busy parking lot,
heading for the market, Edna tried to think more
positively. She would wait to hear what Ernie had to say.
Approaching the automatic doors, she glanced at her
watch, wondering if he might have given up on her and

left.

Inside, sounds of conversation, the blip of electronic scanners and hum of conveyor belts assaulted Edna's ears. Slightly out of breath, she paused, looking around for the deli section and the small eating area he had said she would find. Dodging carts and baggers at the end of the checkout lines, she finally spotted the detective sitting at a small table, a Styrofoam coffee cup in front of him. As she came closer, he stood, relief plain on his face.

"Did you think I wasn't coming?" she asked, unbuttoning her coat.

"It had crossed my mind," he said, indicating she should sit on the anchored swivel chair across from him. "One thing I've learned is that women are never predictable."

She studied his face for a minute, but before she could determine if he was joking or not, he said, "Want some coffee?"

"No, thanks. I'm fine. I've just finished lunch." She slipped off her coat and laid it on the stool beside her before sitting across from him. "I haven't much time, so you'd better finish telling me about Anita. You said her parents died in a car accident. Are you certain it was an accident?" She thought again of Michele's skiing fatality and Lia's hit-and-run.

"It's what the neighbors said. I have no reason to think otherwise."

"Do you know what happened or how it happened?"

"I've been more concerned about finding the daughter. I can get details from her, if I need to know," he said, sounding defensive.

"Another car accident," Edna mused. "Do you think

there might be a connection between the Colliers and Lia's death?" Silently she wondered, *or Michele's death*?

"I don't know what to think yet. I've only been on this case a couple of days. All I know is I can't find Anita Collier. The police are on the lookout for the vehicle that plowed into the Martin woman. I have a friend on the force who will let me know if they find it. My job is to track down Anita, not find the driver who killed Lia." His voice held a note of what Edna felt was desperation.

Prompted by curiosity, she made a mental note to visit the library and see if she could find some back newspapers. A car accident resulting in a double fatality would certainly have appeared in one of the community weekly papers, if not the daily paper. If she was in luck, and Anita had paid the extra expense, she might even find an obituary for the Colliers. Aloud, she said, "You mentioned a great-aunt dying. What's that all about?"

"Elizabeth Collier Maitland. She's the reason my client, her lawyer, has been trying to reach Anita's father."

Edna shook her head. "This is all very confusing."

Leaning forward to rest his forearms on the table between them, Ernie said, "I'll try to tell it like my client told me." He paused for a minute as if to regroup his thoughts before continuing. "The Collier family originally came from upstate New York, somewhere around Rochester, and apparently, they're rich as sin. Elizabeth never had children, and her brother had only the one son. That was Harrington, Anita's father," he added.

"When he was in his early twenties, Harrington had a falling out with the family. My client isn't certain about the details, but Harrington's father disowned his son. Harrington left the area, never to be heard from again."

"How terrible," Edna murmured, thinking how miserable she would be if she lost contact with one of her children.

"Yes, well, apparently Mrs. Maitland has known for some time that Harrington has been living in Denver. For years, she had hopes he would someday contact her, but recently she suffered two heart attacks and can no longer wait for him to make the first move. She wants a reconciliation but figures Harrington must be as pig-headed as his father. As an incentive, she's stipulated in her will that if her nephew comes to see her before she dies, he will inherit her estate, estimated at roughly ten million dollars."

Ernie paused as if to let the amount register with Edna, who merely raised her eyebrows and nodded for him to continue.

"If Harrington refuses to reconcile with his aunt, the estate goes to The Quinn Foundation, an organization for the care of homeless animals, headed by Mrs. Maitland's veterinarian, Louis Quinn. My client says Mrs. Maitland has two dogs, three cats and six exotic birds, and she's worried about their welfare after she's gone. He also says this Quinn fellow has ingratiated himself with the rich widow, and my client doesn't trust the vet as far as he can spit."

Trying to make sense of what she was hearing, Edna said, "But since Harrington is dead, doesn't that already mean Dr. Quinn will inherit everything?"

"My client says not. According to Mrs. Maitland's will, it can be Harrington or, if the aunt survives him, any of his offspring. Obviously, that means Anita, but she must show up in person. That's the kicker. If she doesn't present herself before her great-aunt passes, then the vet gets it all." Ernie paused briefly before continuing. "Because of the old lady's fragile condition, my client hasn't mentioned the nephew's death to her yet. He thinks if we can bring Harrington's daughter to Mrs. Maitland, it might make the news of the nephew's death less of a shock. That's why I have to find Anita as soon as possible. Docs don't give Mrs. Maitland much longer to live."

Edna remembered Grant's concern that Anita was hiding purposely. She thought of Anita's friends and family, too many of them dead under mysterious circumstances. *Is Ernie telling the truth, or is this an elaborate story to win my sympathy and assistance? Is he really working for Mrs. Maitland's lawyer or for Dr. Quinn? Or could he be working for Anita's husband? Does he want to find Anita to send her to New York or to prevent her from getting to her great-aunt's bedside or neither?* Edna's head was beginning to ache as she tried to separate her son's suspicions from this earnest stranger's pleas.

"Why are you doing this?" she finally asked aloud. "If you don't take cases involving people, why are you so determined to pursue this woman? Why not turn it over to the police, report her as a missing person?"

Ernie hesitated, looking at the Styrofoam cup he was mutilating with his fingers. After a long moment he raised his eyes to hers, looking defensive. "Look, I'm not out to stiff anyone, but if I can reunite an old woman with the only relative she's got left, if I can help to make her last days happy, my client will pay me well." He frowned and pursed his lips, looking down at the now demolished cup. In a voice so low that she almost didn't catch the words, he said, "And I can sure use the money right now."

Edna thought about his answer for a few minutes before replying. If his story were true, the important thing was to find Anita and get her to New York. But if Grant's feelings were correct, Anita could be walking into a trap. If Edna were to help Ernie, maybe she could make certain no harm came to the young woman. Remembering Grant's story of how Anita had cared for Michele and Jillian, Edna felt she should repay some of that kindness. If she could help at all, and if there really was a dying great-aunt, Edna wanted to see that Anita got safely to New York. Whatever else was involved, this Mrs. Maitland was the only relative Anita had left. In a moment of fantasy, Edna pictured herself accompanying the young woman to her great-aunt's deathbed.

The thought of flying brought Edna back to her senses. She had been on an airplane only once in her life, and that had been last week. Because of the urgency of her husband's request, she had proven to herself that she could overcome this particular fear, but that didn't mean she'd enjoyed the experience. Forcing the memory from her mind, she said, "Okay. Assuming I won't be able to get any more information out of Grant than you have, how do we go about finding Anita? Where would we even begin to look for her?"

Ernie's face lit up at her implied collusion before his frown reappeared. "That's the odd thing. She seems to be everywhere but nowhere. The only thing I've done so far is leave messages on her answering machine. That's how I knew Grant had changed the recording. Since she hasn't called me back, I don't even know if she's gotten the messages."

"Not calling someone back is not unusual," Edna said.

"I don't return calls if I don't recognize the name. Too many sales people leave messages as if they were long lost friends." She thought for several seconds before continuing. "You've been to her home?" It was more a question than a statement.

"Several times. Her parents' next-door neighbor gave me Anita's address and the picture. She seemed worried. Said Anita had mentioned taking some time off work so she could go through the house, box up personal papers, take clothes to Goodwill. You know, stuff like that. According to the neighbor, Anita wanted to put the house up for sale as quickly as possible, but the neighbor hasn't seen any activity around the place since around the time of the Colliers' funeral. Said she'd tried calling Anita at home and on her cell phone, but she hasn't been able to reach her.

"After talking to the neighbor, I went to Anita's condo and knocked on the door, but there was no answer. I even staked out the place for a few nights. It's a big complex, mostly young singles, lots of comings and goings 'til pretty late. Things pick up again about six in the morning when people start leaving for work. None of the neighbors I talked to pay much attention to other units, so I didn't learn anything from them. I noticed Anita's lights go on and off in different rooms at different times, but my guess is they're on timers."

"What about her mail? Wouldn't that be stacked up or her mailbox overflowing? Maybe you could check with her postal service."

"She rents a post office box. So far, I haven't been able to find out if she's picked up her mail or not or if she requested a hold."

"Maybe she changed her mind about taking time off and has gone back to work. Some people seem to need the distractions of a job after a major tragedy in their lives. Have you found out anything at her office?"

"Before Grant had me thrown out, you mean?" Ernie's eyes twinkled, taking some of the sting out of his words. "Yes, as a matter of fact, I did, but it didn't do me much good. Her paycheck gets deposited automatically, so she doesn't have to come in to pick it up on payday. I checked with the utility companies, but all her bills are paid automatically through her bank." He lowered his face and pinched the bridge of his nose as he shook his head. "I swear people's lives run on autopilot these days."

Edna nodded in agreement before speaking. "So what makes you think she's missing? She might be working. From what my son tells me, she covers a wide and pretty desolate territory."

"That's where you can help me out. If you can't get Grant to tell you where she is, maybe you could go to his office and ask around. See if anyone's heard from her or maybe get names of some of the customers she would contact?" He smiled ruefully. "I'd go myself, but thanks to Grant, I'm no longer welcome around his workplace."

While she was thinking about how she might arrange to go to Grant's office and spy behind his back, the phone in her purse began to play the jaunty little tune he had selected when he'd programmed his family's numbers into the instrument. Looking at her watch as she reached for the cell, she was astounded to realize it was nearing three o'clock, the time Jillian usually got home from school. Feeling certain it was Karissa calling, Edna didn't look at the caller's ID before answering.

"Yes, dear, I'm on my way home right now."

"Edna?" Albert's voice, sounding confused. "Is that you, Edna?"

"Albert?" Surprised to hear from her husband in the middle of the afternoon, Edna was momentarily at a loss for words.

"What do you mean you're on your way home? Where are you?"

"I'm at the grocery store near Grant's house. I thought you were Karissa."

Just then a young woman approached their table, stooping to pick Ernie's hat up off the floor. "Is this yours, sir," she asked.

"Oh, yes." Ernie said, retrieving the crumpled item from the woman. "Must have dropped it. Thanks."

"Who's that?" Albert's voice sounded in Edna's ear. "Doesn't sound like Grant. Who are you with at the grocery store?"

She didn't want to go into a lengthy explanation right then, so she improvised. "Sorry, dear, but you seem to be breaking up. Let me get back to the house. I'll call you later." Without waiting for a reply, she pushed the disconnect button.

Five

Edna agreed to let Ernie drive her back to the house, although she worried that either Karissa or Jillian would see her with him. If word got back to Grant, he would be very angry. *Really, I must have my own car*, she thought as they neared her son's address.

"Do you think you can scout around Office Plus for me?" Ernie's voice broke into her thoughts as he stopped in front of the house.

Guilt about being with him in the first place made her hesitate at the thought of sneaking around Grant's place of business, but only until she considered the missing young woman. She held a picture of Lia in her mind—had the funeral been only this morning?—and coupled it with the small photo of Anita that Ernie had given to her. Mentally, she put the two young women side by side with her own youngest daughter Starling. What would she do if Starling were missing? Edna's heart lurched.

Anita needs to be found. I don't care what Grant's motive is for keeping quiet or Ernie's for tracking her, I want her found. I want to know she's alive and well, Edna thought.

Anxious to get away, but realizing there was still much she wanted to know, she said, "Perhaps I can arrange something. How will I contact you?"

"I'll have to call you. I'm in the process of changing my mobile service, and I don't have my new phone yet."

"Do you have an office?"

"It's in the basement of my house, but I'm out most of the time. You won't get me there."

"Don't you have an answering machine? I could leave a message."

"My wife usually answers the phone, but she's been sick lately, and I don't want her disturbed. No, I'd better call you."

Wondering if he were making himself purposely unavailable, Edna pulled a scrap of paper from her tote bag and scribbled down her cell phone number.

Pocketing the bit of paper, Ernie grabbed her arm as she was about to get out of the car. "I'll put a list together of things I want you to find out. Can you meet me back at Safeway in the morning, say around nine o'clock?"

"I'll try." Edna twisted from his grasp and got out of the car. She hurried up the walk, entering the house quietly. She didn't want to disturb Karissa if she was sleeping, but she wondered if she might be watching from the bedroom window. Going directly to the kitchen, Edna had time to clean up the lunch dishes before Jillian came bursting into the house, calling, "I'm home" at the top of her lungs.

"Okay, okay," Edna rushed to the living room, drying her hands on a small towel. "I think everyone in the neighborhood heard you. You probably woke up Karissa."

"Nah, she doesn't sleep all that much. I'll go check."

Before Edna could stop her, Jillian bounded down the hall and into the master bedroom, yelling, "Hey, Karissa. I'm home."

Edna heard Karissa's answering voice but couldn't make out the words as she followed her granddaughter down the hall. Approaching the bedroom, she heard the two laughing and chattering. Unbidden anger flared at the sound. Michele should be the one in that bedroom. It wasn't fair. Edna's heart ached thinking of Jillian's mother not being there to listen to her daughter talking excitedly about her day at school.

It may have been these thoughts that caused her to speak more abruptly than she had meant to when she entered the room. "Jillian, quiet down. You know Karissa mustn't be agitated. Sorry, Karissa."

Karissa said she didn't mind, she looked forward to seeing Jillian after school, but Edna said the child needed to get some fresh air after being inside. "Jillian, come with me. We'll go out and play. It's too nice a day to stay inside."

Good naturedly, Jillian skipped from the room and went to change her clothes while Edna brought Karissa a cup of tea and some cookies. Then, donning a light windbreaker and her wide-brimmed hat, she went out to join her granddaughter in the backyard.

"Play Frisbee with me, Gramma," Jillian shouted as Edna appeared on the deck.

"I'm not sure I can. I've never done it before."

"I'll teach you. Come on. It's fun."

Jillian spun the plastic saucer at Edna who, to the surprise of them both, caught the toy in mid-air. Laughing, Edna tried to throw it back but only managed to spin it sideways, slamming it into the ground.

"That's okay, Gramma. I'll show you how." Jillian ran after the Frisbee before joining Edna in the middle of the yard. "See. Like this."

For the next half hour or so, Jillian taught Edna how to flex and flick her wrist so the Frisbee would sail evenly and smoothly through the air. Once, the disc caught on a sudden breeze and was carried into the neighboring yard. Edna stood on tiptoe, looking over the wooden privacy fence, watching as Jillian entered the yard and threw the Frisbee back. The youngster was full of energy and soon had Edna panting with exhaustion.

"Enough," she finally cried, laughing and stumbling toward the glider on the redwood deck.

Jillian came to stand before her, saying in her serious child's tones, "You're doing really great, Gramma. You can't stop now."

"Thank you, Jillybean, but I need to sit for a minute. I'll play some more later." Thinking of how she might get her granddaughter to calm down a little before dinner, she said, "If you'll bring me a pencil and some paper, I'll draw a picture of my cat for you."

"All ri-i-ight," Jillian shouted, drawing out the last word, as she went running into the house, returning moments later with a pencil, a spiral-bound notepad and several crayons clutched in her fist. Wiggling onto the glider next to Edna, she thrust the materials at her grandmother.

While Edna took the pencil and began to swipe a series of curved lines on the paper, she asked Jillian to tell her about school, listening to the child's description of her third-grade teacher, Mr. Cameron, and smiling to herself over stories Jillian told of her school friends. When the pencil drawing of Benjamin was finished, Edna took an orange crayon and added color to the cat's back and head.

"Is that really what he looks like?" Jillian took the picture onto her lap and studied it.

"Yes. He's a big ginger cat. Very friendly and very

smart."

"Did you get him when he was a kitten?"

"No. He was already a year old when he came to live with us. Your grandfather and I adopted him from an animal shelter."

"I want a kitten." Jillian stated firmly.

From the expression on her granddaughter's face, Edna wondered if she hadn't gotten into a conversation that had already been decided between Jillian and her parents. Taking the notepad, she flipped to a clean page and began to draw again. "Have you asked your daddy for a kitten?"

"Yes. No. Not exactly." Jillian played with the zipper on her jacket, not looking up at Edna. "When Mommy was still alive, I asked for a dog, but they said no."

Edna felt an overwhelming sadness when Jillian mentioned Michele. "Your mother was allergic to dogs and cats. Their fur made her sneeze," Edna said.

"I remember." The little voice was quieter now.

Trying to keep the conversation light, Edna said, "What else do you remember about your mother, Jillybean?"

"Everything." Enthusiasm came back into Jillian's voice. "I hold her picture and talk to her every night before Daddy turns off my light. I tell her about school and stuff. I know she can hear me, even though she's in heaven and I can't see her anymore."

The lump in Edna's throat kept her from responding. Instead, she turned the picture she'd just finished so that Jillian could see it. Edna had an artist's eye and a memory for detail, talents which had recently helped her to identify a murderer. Now these talents were being put to work to bring happiness to her granddaughter.

The little girl's eyes widened. "That's me and Mommy." Smiling broadly, she looked up at Edna. "That's us, isn't it?"

"Yes, dear. That's you and your mommy." Edna had drawn Michele's face from memory and, cheek-to-cheek, had added Jillian as she was today, with her reddish brown braids and a smattering of freckles across her nose.

Before Edna could stop her, Jillian jumped off the glider and headed for the sliding glass door, waving the picture. "I'm gonna go show Karissa," she said, dashing into the house.

"Oh, no," Edna moaned aloud, pushing herself up to follow her granddaughter. "Wait, Jillian," she called, but the youngster was already down the hall.

As Edna entered the bedroom, she saw Jillian kneeling beside the bed. The child's stepmother, having to lie on her side most of the time, was holding the picture at arm's length and saying, "It's a wonderful drawing, Jilly. We'll have to get a nice frame to put it in."

"Oh, yes. Can we?" Jillian looked over her shoulder at Edna.

Edna studied Karissa, worried that she might be upset at the image of Michele, but she needn't have been concerned. Karissa's look was soft and smiling. "Tell you what, Jilly," she said to her stepdaughter, "after the baby is born, we'll all go shopping and pick out a perfect frame."

"Awesome," Jillian cried and, taking the picture, ran from the room.

"I hope you're not upset by my drawing," Edna said by way of apology, sitting on the edge of a chair near the bed.

"Not at all. I think Jillian needs to keep her mother's

memory alive as long as possible. It's a good likeness."

"Oh, did you know Michele?" Edna had somehow supposed that Grant's two wives had never met.

"Not really. I met her once when she came to the office." Without pausing, Karissa said, "You draw people so well. Did you take lessons?"

Realizing her new daughter-in-law wanted to change the subject, Edna told Karissa that she had been sketching faces since she'd been about Jillian's age. "I drew pictures to entertain my little sister when she broke her leg one summer and couldn't get out to play. I guess I just had a knack for it," Edna said.

Not comfortable talking about herself, she bent to retrieve a couple of magazines from the floor beside the bed before rising and picking up the empty teacup and cookie plate. She was grateful that Karissa seemed so understanding of Jillian's need to remember her mother. "Can I get you anything else before I start dinner?"

"No, thanks. I feel guilty having you wait on me like this."

Edna smiled. "Don't you bother about it. After all, that's what I'm here for. Take advantage of it while you can. You'll be wishing for more bed time once that baby of yours arrives."

Karissa smiled and leaned back into her pillows as Jillian came bounding into the room again, carrying two dolls and a tiny suitcase. "Play dolls, Karissa?" she asked, climbing up onto the bed without waiting for a reply.

"Jillian, I don't think ... " began Edna, but Karissa stopped her.

"It's all right. I want to play. It gets pretty boring just lying here with nothing to do but read or watch TV. I've gone through all my magazines at least five times."

Edna was about to suggest she bring Karissa a book to read when Jillian spoke up.

"You play too, Gramma," she commanded, opening the little suitcase and dumping doll clothes and accessories onto the bed.

Looking at her watch, Edna said, "No. You two play. Your father will be home soon, and I've got to make supper."

In the kitchen she rummaged through cupboards, looking for something to go with the hamburger she had taken out of the freezer that morning. She hadn't had to cook an evening meal in Grant's home yet and was anxious to make a good wholesome supper for the family. Grant had brought food home the last two nights, Kentucky Fried Chicken one night and pizza the next. Edna was ready for a decent meal, not something preprocessed and packaged on an assembly line.

She didn't find potatoes in the kitchen but did locate a box of white rice. The canned goods consisted of several varieties of beans, including chili, kidney, pinto and garbanzo. There were cans of tomatoes, too, mostly diced with jalapeno peppers. The shelves seemed full of items unfamiliar to Edna's typical type of cooking. Finally, she discovered a jar of beef bouillon granules and decided to make a meatloaf and serve it with rice and gravy. Spotting a head of lettuce in the refrigerator, she thought a leafy salad would do for their green vegetable.

Next, she looked through the spice jars but couldn't find much she was familiar with there either. Chili powder, Tabasco and two other kinds of hot sauce. There was oregano, but she wasn't making spaghetti. Where was the thyme or rosemary or sage? She didn't want to use salt, certain Karissa would be on a low sodium diet, so she finally flavored the ground beef with a dash of Worcestershire and some seasoned croutons that she crushed and mixed into the meat.

Having set the table, made a lettuce salad with an oil-and-vinegar dressing, and prepared a mock gravy with bouillon, flour and water, Edna looked at the clock. The meatloaf would be done in five minutes. Grant was late. She had always served supper at six for her family, and it was almost that now. Deciding not to break that long-time habit and thinking she would warm Grant's meal for him when he got home, she was on her way down the hall to ask Jillian to wash her hands when she heard the phone ring and Karissa pick it up.

Edna entered the bedroom in time to hear her daughter-in-law say, "Okay, we'll see you when you get home." She pushed a button on the cordless phone and handed it to Jillian as she looked up at Edna. "That was Grant. He has to work late tonight and said to go ahead and eat without him. He'll grab something near the office."

Edna hoped she disguised her disappointment. She was getting to know Karissa better but still was more comfortable with her daughter-in-law when Grant was around. When the two women were alone, the conversation felt stilted. Edna needed time to get to know Grant's second wife before she would feel like having anything more than superficial conversation. Oh, well, nothing to do but put on a good face.

"Will you wash up for supper, please," she said to her granddaughter. To her daughter-in-law, she held out a hand. "May I help you up?"

"Thanks, Edna." Karissa put out her hands, and together they maneuvered her to a sitting position on the edge of the bed. "I'll use the bathroom and join you at the table in a minute," she said, dismissing Edna with a shy smile.

Retreating down the hall, Edna savored the warmth of Karissa's smile. The more she was around this daughter-in-law, the more she liked her. Oh, but she missed Michele and the easy camaraderie they had shared. As she entered the kitchen, the oven's timer went off, and Edna had no more time to dwell on the past.

Determined to be cheerful and draw Karissa out, Edna regaled her dinner companions with stories of her children growing up and some of the family traditions they had enjoyed. Jillian and Karissa were delighted with the tales of Grant as a young boy.

Later in the meal conversation centered around Jillian's friends, both at school and in the neighborhood. Finishing the last bite of salad on her plate, Edna was thinking how much she had enjoyed the last half hour when she noticed that Karissa had hardly touched the food.

"Is something wrong?" Edna asked, concerned.

"No, no. Everything's fine. I guess I'm not very hungry." Karissa put down her fork, not looking at Edna. "I think I'll just get back to bed."

"You can lean on me, Karissa," Jillian said, jumping up and standing beside her stepmother while Karissa, after pushing herself up from the table, put a hand on the girl's shoulder for support.

As Edna cleared the dishes, loaded the dishwasher and put away the leftover food, she thought about her son and wondered what was so important that he couldn't make it home to have an evening meal with his family. *Does this happen often?* she wondered. She surprised herself by thinking he might not be at the office at all but out somewhere. Visiting with Anita, perhaps? If only she had a car, she could drive over to Office Plus and at least see if his Celica was in the parking lot.

Mentally scolding herself for even thinking that her son was capable of such underhanded actions, she added soap to the trap in the dishwasher and turned it on. She then went to investigate what the other females in the family were up to. When she reached the open door to the master bedroom, she saw that Jillian had a book open and was reading quietly to her stepmother. Edna stood in the doorway and watched the two, happy to see how well they got along.

Jillian finished the page and was about to begin another when Karissa stopped her. "You've got school tomorrow, kiddo. It's time to get ready for bed."

"Ahh, just one more page. Pleeease," Jillian begged.

"You know the rules," Karissa said lightly but firmly. She caught Edna's eye as she said this. Giving Edna a wink, she smiled back at Jillian. "Maybe tomorrow you can read a story to your grandmother."

"Okay." Reluctantly but obediently, Jillian gave her stepmother's cheek a kiss and scrambled off the bed. She then ran to Edna who bent to receive a good night hug and kiss.

Edna watched the child race down the hall to her room, turning back to Karissa in time to see a look of pain cross her daughter-in-law's face. All thoughts of Jillian flew from her head.

"What is it, dear? What's wrong?"

Karissa smiled weakly, sweat glazing her forehead. "The baby's very active tonight," she said, holding onto her enlarged belly. "I think it's trying to kick its way out." She attempted a laugh that turned quickly into a grimace.

"Oh, dear," Edna said, chuckling to ease the tension, but with considerable sympathy. "I remember those days." She went to the master bathroom and brought back a damp face cloth that she used to gently wipe her daughter-in-law's brow. Then, she refilled Karissa's water glass and asked if there were anything else she could do.

Tears glimmered in Karissa's eyes as she replied with a soft smile. "Not unless you can get my husband to come home." With that, she closed her eyes and burrowed her head into a pillow.

Sensing the young woman wanted to be alone with her unhappiness, Edna left the room, quietly closing the door. The pleasure of the evening was gone.

In her own room she picked up her knitting bag and returned to the living room. She was making a baby's blanket of alternating green and yellow squares. Grant and Karissa had told the family they didn't know the baby's sex. They wanted to be surprised. They also informed anyone who asked that no, they hadn't chosen a name yet either. Karissa believed that an appropriate name would occur to her only after she held her baby in her arms and looked into his or her face. Her mother had named her in that manner and so Karissa would do the same with her own child.

Edna sat on the couch, knitting with the television on, although she couldn't have said what she was watching. She had turned it on primarily to hear other voices. She was counting rows to determine if she needed to change colors, when she heard a sound behind her. Turning abruptly and dropping her needles in the process, she looked into her granddaughter's worried eyes.

"Jillybean, whatever's the matter?"

"Why didn't you come say goodnight to me?" Jillian's mouth pouted and her eyes looked concerned.

"Oh, Sweetie, I'm so sorry. I didn't know you were waiting for me."

"Daddy's not here, so I thought you'd tuck me in." She hurled herself into Edna's lap and hugged her tightly.

As Edna gently rocked the child back and forth, a thought popped into her head. Without giving it much thought, she said as if merely curious, "Jillian, would you tell me about your friend Anita?"

The little girl lifted her head and looked into Edna's eyes. "Daddy doesn't want me to talk to anyone about Anita."

"Why not?" Edna was surprised at this statement.

"Because."

"I don't think he'd mind if you talked to me. Do you?"

Brow wrinkled in a frown, Jillian thought for several seconds before finally shaking her head. "I guess not. I guess he didn't mean I couldn't talk to you, Gramma." She smiled and rested her head on Edna's shoulder.

"When did you see her last?" Edna asked, stroking the child's hair.

Jillian seemed to think very hard before shrugging. "I don't know. It was a really long time ago. Before Grampa came to visit us."

Edna realized how silly her question had been. Albert had arrived in Denver almost two weeks ago. The time prior to that would be fuzzy to an eight-year-old. She tried again. "When you saw her last, did she seem different to you? I mean, did she act differently?"

"Nope." Jillian shook her head emphatically and gave a little giggle. "Anita's fun." Then her small face took on a quizzical look. "Do you think she's with Mommy, Gramma?"

Shuddering inwardly that the child had voiced the question that had been haunting Edna herself, she said, "What makes you ask that?"

"Oh, nothing. It's just that she used to come here all the time and now she doesn't."

"You know," Edna said carefully, "her own mommy and daddy recently went to heaven. Maybe she just went away for a while, on a trip perhaps." Then, changing the subject, she gave Jillian a hug, lifted the child off her lap and stood, holding out a hand. "Come. Let's get you to bed. You've got a busy day of school ahead of you."

Jillian giggled. "That sounded just like when you talk to Daddy." She lowered her voice and made Edna laugh by saying, "You've got a busy day at the office ahead of you, Grant."

Finally getting Jillian to bed, Edna was about to return to her knitting when she remembered she hadn't taken out the trash. Going through to the kitchen and beyond to the laundry room where she had left a tied, white plastic bag, she opened the door into the large two-car garage.

One side of the garage was empty except for Jillian's pink bicycle and a few toys. That's where Grant's Celica would go, if he ever bothered to bring it in. He seemed to prefer parking it in the driveway. The other side held their larger vehicle beneath a fitted cover, the car they would use for family outings, Edna assumed. A large metal container stood against the wall at the rear of the big van, along with bins for recycling paper and aluminum. Once she had disposed of the kitchen rubbish, replaced the lid and was turning to go back into the house, she took another look at the canvas hiding the dark blue 4-Runner. Why would Grant cover the car when it was in the garage?

At that moment, Lia Martin's face popped into Edna's mind. She had been killed by a dark-colored SUV, according to the witness. Edna's heart began to pound. She reached out to touch the cloth but pulled back before her fingers brushed the fabric. Absurd. Grant wasn't a killer. There's a perfectly good explanation. Still, it wouldn't hurt to look, to make certain. With growing concern, she moved cautiously to the front of the vehicle and examined the covering. She could detect no variations in the shape of the hood, not like one side was caved in or anything like that. Again, she reached out her hand, and this time, she took hold of the cloth.

"What are you doing?"

She jumped back from the car and spun around, her hand flying to her heart. Grant was standing in the laundry room doorway, holding a pizza box.

Six

Pressing a hand over her rapidly beating heart, Edna gasped. "You scared the daylights out of me."

"What are you doing out here, Mother?" Grant repeated the question as he stood aside to let her re-enter the house. "Why are you messing around the car?"

Walking back into the kitchen, she was glad her back was to her son as she thought frantically of what to tell him. She felt guilty for thinking even for a second that he could be capable of killing someone or helping another to cover up a murder, and she was horrified he might somehow read her mind.

"Well," she began slowly, deciding she couldn't lie but perhaps she would tell only part of what she'd been thinking, "I was curious as to why you bother to cover the car when it's in the garage."

Putting the pizza box on the kitchen counter and opening a cupboard above his head, Grant pulled down two small plates before turning to answer. "Oh, that. It's to keep Jillian from scratching the paint. She plays out there sometimes when the weather's bad, especially when the wind picks up. She says she doesn't like it when the wind blows dirt in her eyes." Grant grinned at Edna as he reached around her to grab some napkins out of a red plastic holder on the counter. "Can't say as I blame her."

Becoming aware of what her son was doing, she said, "Haven't you had supper yet?"

He looked sheepishly at the box, plates and napkins in his hand. "Sure, I grabbed a bite earlier, but Karissa called to say she'd share some pizza with me if I brought one home."

"I made a perfectly good meatloaf for dinner. Karissa hardly touched it."

"Guess her appetite's returned." Grant hurried from the kitchen. Over his shoulder he called, "Good night, Mother. See you in the morning."

She didn't know whether to be relieved that Grant wasn't going to press her further as to her actions in the garage, put off that her son had dismissed her so abruptly, or concerned about Karissa's eating habits. Turning off lights as she went, she walked through the living room and slowly down the hall to her own room. She donned her nightgown and slipped between the sheets, her head cluttered with many questions, some big, some small, but all promising to give her a restless night.

Why had Grant married Karissa so soon after Michele's death? What did Karissa think of her new mother-in-law? Was Jillian happy with her stepmother? She certainly seemed to be, Edna decided the answer to at least that one question.

Why was it so hard for her to accept her new daughter-in-law? Had Karissa not been hungry at dinnertime, or did she not like the meatloaf, or ... and at this thought, Edna almost sat straight up in bed. *Does she resent my being here?* Mulling over this idea for several minutes, she finally decided she must have a serious talk with Karissa very soon.

Restlessly, she turned on her side and bunched the pillow beneath her head, trying to think of something neutral, something that would allow her to relax, when out of nowhere Anita's face popped into her head. She turned over onto her other side, punched the pillow, and stared wide-eyed into the darkness. No other answers came to her that night, and eventually, she managed to get a few hours of fitful sleep.

Rising early the next morning, Edna found herself alone with Grant at the breakfast table and decided that the subject of what she had been doing in the garage could be used to her advantage. Hoping to get the conversation over with before Jillian or Karissa joined them, she glanced at her son to see what kind of mood he might be in. He appeared to be in fairly good spirits, sipping a cup of coffee while he idly turned pages of the newspaper he had spread out on the table beside his plate.

Carrying a platter of scrambled eggs and toast to the table, Edna sat in the chair to his right.

"I'd like to talk to you about your extra car," she said, picking up her own coffee cup.

"Sure." Grant folded the paper and studied the food on his plate. "As a matter of fact, Karissa asked me to talk to you about some sort of transportation. She thinks you're going stir crazy." He rose and went into the kitchen, burrowing in the refrigerator for a minute before returning with a jar of salsa. Edna watched in amazement as he spooned the spicy, chunky tomato substance onto his eggs and began to eat. After swallowing a mouthful, he seemed satisfied and turned his attention to her.

"I thought there would be more for me to do while Karissa's lying down, but the meals, housework and laundry take so very little of my time. It would be nice to be able to get around a bit. I could do more of the grocery shopping, particularly since you don't seem to have much free time these days."

"The 4-Runner is Karissa's." Grant popped another forkful of salsa and egg into his mouth, seeming to ponder something.

"Actually, I wasn't talking about the SUV. I'd prefer to drive something smaller. Would she mind if you took her vehicle to work so I could use your Celica?" When Grant didn't immediately respond, she hurried on. "I don't always need to be right here in the house, you know. Karissa sleeps a lot, and I don't think it can be very peaceful to have someone else roaming around in your house. I wouldn't go far, and she has my cell number if she needs me."

"Dad doesn't like the idea of you driving around Denver by yourself. He thinks you might get lost or something."

"Your father doesn't need to be worried about what I might or might not do," she responded. "When he was here, I had someone to talk to. We played cards and went for walks. We had the rental car to go for groceries."

"I'm sure Karissa would talk to you or even play cards. She likes board games."

"But I need to get out of the house now and then, and she needs time to herself, as well. You said she suggested talking to me about transportation. She might be getting tired of my always hanging about." Thinking in part of her meeting with Ernie later that morning, Edna was not going to be swayed from her purpose.

"Where would you go? You don't know the area." Grant said. "I don't want to be worrying about you, Mother."

"As I said, I could do the food shopping, and I'd like to go to the library occasionally. I could visit Jillybean's school." She hesitated, remembering her desire to go by Grant's office the night before. If he had something to hide, maybe he wouldn't want her driving around where she might spot him. She glanced at him from the corner of her eye. "I'd also like to drive over and see where you work."

Grant straightened and his face seemed to light up. "That's a great idea. I'd like to show you around. Actually, I'd been planning on driving you over and back myself, but I've been so busy." He hesitated before adding, "Somehow, I didn't think you'd be interested."

"Of course, I'm interested." She was surprised her son would think otherwise, but before he lost track of the main subject, she added, "So you agree that I can use your car?"

Almost as if on cue, Karissa waddled into the kitchen with Jillian close behind. The two new arrivals took seats at the table, and Karissa reached for the platter to help Jillian and then herself to eggs over which she liberally poured the salsa. "Have you been talking about a car for Edna?" she asked, looking at Grant.

"My mother wants to come see where I work. She wants to use the Toyota."

Karissa's eyes brightened as she turned to Edna. "What a good idea. You've got to be bored stiff around here." Turning back to Grant, she said, "What about the SUV? She could use that."

"I thought she'd be better off in the Celica, and I'll take the 4-Runner to work."

"Fine with me." Karissa picked up a fork, smiling across the table at Edna.

"Gramma can drive me to school," Jillian chimed in

before shoveling eggs and salsa into her mouth.

Edna laughed. "I certainly could if you show me the way."

The meal ended happily with Edna going off to school with Jillian, leaving Grant to spend more time over another cup of coffee with his wife. With Grant's explicit, written directions, Edna would later meet him at Office Plus for lunch and a quick tour. As she started the engine and backed out of the driveway with Jillian safely buckled into the back seat, Edna thought she knew what it must feel like to be newly released from prison.

The wind, so strong the day before, had stopped and the sun was shining. Not a cloud broke the expanse of blue sky. Edna thought even the light coat she had put on might be too warm. She would have sworn it was the middle of summer if it weren't for the gold and red leaves covering the trees along the route to the elementary school.

After dropping Jillian off and waving to the crossing-guard on duty, Edna drove to Safeway to meet Ernie and tell him the good news, not only about the car but about wangling an invitation to Grant's office. It was five minutes past nine when she sat down across from him at the small table they had shared the previous afternoon.

"This is everything you want me to find out?" she said, glancing up from the list he had handed her. He had gone to get coffee for them both while she read the list and had just returned.

"Yes, find out anything you can about Anita, who might have seen her and when. What did they talk about? Where she goes when she takes off for a few days."

"And about her territory," Edna offered. "I should probably find out something about the work she does."

"Sure. See if you can get a list of her accounts or at least some customers she visits regularly."

"I might not have much success, but I'll do what I can." Stopping to think over what she was preparing to do, she wondered about her own sanity. How was she possibly going to pull this off?

Ernie ignored her hesitation and self-doubts. "Anything you can get will help. If we get even one customer's name, it could lead us to others."

"Shall I meet you back here this afternoon? I don't know how long I'll be."

"No, I've got a few things to do myself. I want to run a background check on Anita's husband." Ernie pulled a small spiral notepad from his inside jacket pocket and flipped it open. "Rice Ryan." He looked at her with an amused expression. "Who would name a kid Rice?"

Edna shrugged, smiling back. "I've heard worse. Maybe it was his mother's maiden name."

"Could be," Ernie conceded and bent over the pad, making a notation as he added, "I'm also going to check into the accident that killed her parents."

Edna was silent for a minute, watching Ernie scribble notes. She hesitated, feeling as if she might be imposing on this new relationship. But who better to ask and she desperately wanted to know. "Could you ... would you ...?" she faltered before finally spitting out the words. "Can you check something for me?"

He raised his head and looked suspiciously at her, hesitating before responding. "Check on what?"

"I'd like to know what happened to my daughter-in-law, Grant's first wife Michele."

He seemed to squirm in his seat. "I've already begun

checking on your son and his past, especially the women."

She felt her stomach knot at the thought of her son under investigation. Thinking about it for a minute or two, she nodded slowly. "I guess that makes sense, since you think he knows where Anita is. Well," she concluded matter-of-factly, "I'd like to know whatever you can tell me about Michele's accident."

"Do you want to know the details? From what I gather, she was skiing too fast, went out of control and hit a tree. End of story."

"Is it?" She stared into his eyes. "Can you tell me without a doubt that Michele's death really was accidental?"

He picked up the pad and shoved it back into his jacket pocket as he held Edna's gaze steadily. "I'll talk to a few people and make sure, but I believe it was."

"Thank you." She rose, picking up her coat and tote bag from the seat beside her. "I have to do some shopping and get home to make Karissa's lunch before I meet Grant at his office."

"Okay." Ernie got up too and slapped his crumpled cloth hat onto his head. "I'll call you."

For the next half hour she walked through the aisles of the grocery store, looking for items similar to what she had seen in the cupboards at Grant's home, checking particularly the Mexican food section and reading recipes on the backs of cans and boxes. A stranger to this particular style of cooking, she was unenlightened as to what a tortilla was or an enchilada or a burrito, so she picked up only a few staples like milk, cheese and a box of macaroni before leaving the store. When she arrived home, she found Karissa lying on the sofa, flipping through one of the magazines Edna had picked up from the bedroom floor and left on the coffee table in the living room.

"How are you feeling?" Putting the groceries away and coming back to the living room, she felt guilty she hadn't been there to help Karissa to the couch.

Karissa smiled up at her as she tossed the magazine back onto the low table. "I'm a little more comfortable today, thanks. Grant made sure I was safely settled before he left. He worries too much." She made a face as if to say how absurd it was, but Edna could see a twinkle in her eyes.

"Are you hungry?" Edna asked, while wondering how to begin the talk she knew she must have with her daughter-in-law.

The look in Karissa's eyes turned wary. "Maybe a little. Are you going to make lunch?"

"I'm going to try, but first I think I'll need some instruction from you." She sat in an armchair facing Karissa. "Is there something special you'd like? Keep in mind that you'll probably have to tell me how to make it."

Karissa's lovely burst of laughter prompted Edna to join in. Then her daughter-in-law began to describe various Mexican, Asian and Middle Eastern foods to Edna and explain the family's preference for different kinds of rice, beans, and spicy dishes. At one point, Edna excused herself, went to get paper and pencil, and began to take notes and ask questions. A happy half hour went by before she finally went into the kitchen with directions on how to make nachos with jalapeno cheese.

Seven

After preparing Karissa's lunch so she needed only to warm it in the microwave when she was hungry, Edna helped her daughter-in-law settle more comfortably on the living room sofa and put magazines, blanket and cell phone within easy reach. When she was assured Karissa had everything she wanted, Edna arranged a navy blue hat on her gray curls and asked one last time, "Sure you'll be okay?"

Karissa's eyes twinkled over the top of her magazine. "I'll be fine. Really. I'm glad you're getting out. You'll like the Office Plus building. It's modern. Lots of glass, so it's bright and cheerful inside."

Edna smiled. "That's nice. I think, if I had to work in an office, I'd like it to be airy with lots of light."

"Oh, if you run into Wendy Fuller, say hi for me, will you? She was my supervisor."

"Wendy Fuller," Edna repeated, committing the name to memory, as she slipped into her coat. "I'll do that." She opened the front door, gave Karissa a little wave and said, "You'll probably enjoy having the house to yourself for a while."

Karissa buried her face behind the magazine but not before Edna saw the corners of her lips curving upwards.

Twenty minutes later Edna pulled the Celica into a parking space marked Visitor in front of a three-story building that did indeed seem to be built of glass.

Gleaming in the sunlight, the windows appeared almost fluid, like water in a clear pond. She approached tall double doors and pulled one open with surprising ease, finding herself in a large room with a high ceiling and ahead of her, a waist-high semicircular receptionist's counter. Grant, partly turned toward the front doors with one hip perched on the wooden structure, was talking to the young woman seated behind the desk. He turned and straightened as Edna strode across the marble floor of the lobby.

"Be back in an hour, Nina," he called over his shoulder as he took Edna's elbow and escorted her back the way she had come. "We can walk to the restaurant, if you're up for it. It's only a couple blocks away."

Temperatures were in the mid-sixties, but with no wind blowing the air felt warmer. *Dry heat,* she thought, enjoying the feel of the sun on her back as she listened and responded to Grant's small talk.

Weggies was a bustling place where customers stood in line to order sandwiches, soups and salads. The few people ahead of them moved forward quickly, and before she could read any of the overhead signs listing menu items, Edna was greeted by a cashier in a white polo shirt with the restaurant's logo emblazoned on the breast pocket.

"What'll you have?" he asked in a cheerful baritone.

She was accustomed to sit-down-and-be-served eateries where she could spend time looking over the menu, but she decided the service line was very practical and efficient for busy working people who needed to get back to an office. However, at that moment, she felt rushed with the young man drumming his fingers on the counter and a line of people backing up behind her.

"I think you'd like the turkey with tomato, avocado and lettuce." Grant came to her rescue, and at her nod, he ordered and paid for both of them. As her son put his arm around her shoulders and walked her forward, she wondered if a more relaxed atmosphere might be easier on the digestion.

By the time they reached the end of the long, cafeteria-style food line, their sandwiches were waiting on bright orange trays. Grant picked them both up, led her to a line of beverage dispensing machines, filled two large plastic glasses with water, then motioned her to a small table near the middle of the busy room.

She was glad to sit down but still felt harried and a little breathless. She waited in silence while Grant put their plates and glasses on the table and handed their trays to a passing busboy. Mother and son were silent until they had taken the first bites of their sandwiches. Slightly more relaxed, she finally sat back in her chair. "I think Karissa's a lovely girl," she said, opening the topic carefully.

Grant eyed her over his chicken-breast-on-Kaiser-roll, a slight look of surprise on his face. "Thank you, Mother. I think she's pretty special myself." He grinned.

Edna smiled back. "You've never told me how you two met."

His grin faded but didn't disappear. It made him look sad for a moment. "I guess we've needed this talk."

"I … " she began, but he held up a hand, palm toward her.

"Please, let me finish first," he said. "I'd like you to understand, and I'm sorry I haven't been brave enough to bring up the subject myself." He looked sheepish for an instant before continuing. "I know you loved Michele very much, and I did, too," he hurried to add. Staring off to one side, he seemed unaware of others around them. "Actually, I didn't realize how much until she was gone."

"Then, why ..." Edna began, but he stopped her again with a raised hand.

"Why marry Karissa? Or why marry so soon after Michele's accident?"

She wondered why he hesitated before uttering the word accident. What had he been about to say if not accident? His voice interrupted her thoughts.

"I won't lie to you, Mother. Michele and I had grown apart. She was so ... so ... headstrong," he finally blurted out. "She wasn't a restful person, not like Karissa. Not at all gentle or understanding." He looked down at the remainder of his chicken sandwich and pushed the plate away. "I think if it hadn't been for Jillian, Michele and I would have split years ago. I do miss her but more like an old friend than a wife."

Folding his arms on the table and leaning forward, keeping his voice low, he said, "I know Michele wasn't totally to blame. I was at fault, too. I think I was too tame for her. She had a wild, reckless streak. I think that's what first attracted me to her, but it's also what started to come between us." He frowned, shaking his head. "I thought she would settle down a little when Jillian came along, but she didn't. I liked staying at home, but she always wanted to go out. I work long hours sometimes, and she wasn't happy about that. Nothing seemed to be working for us anymore. I don't even know when things really started to fall apart."

"Were you seeing Karissa before ..." Edna couldn't

quite get the right words out.

"You mean, did I cheat on Michele? No. Never." His gaze was steady, and Edna felt he was telling the truth. "Karissa and I ate together in the lunch room at the office." His lips twitched and his eyes lit up. "That's about as blatant and intimate as our relationship got. Sometimes we were the only ones in there because we ate later than everyone else. She filled in on the switchboard at noon, so sometimes she wouldn't have lunch until after one. Most of the time, I forget about eating until I need another cup of coffee. We started talking one afternoon." His eyes dropped to the tabletop as he was obviously caught up in his memories.

After a moment's pause, he looked up, and his eyes were serious. "When her mother was dying of cancer, Karissa became involved with a local support group and still spends a lot of time helping families of cancer patients learn to cope with the disease. Losing her mother hit her hard. They were very close."

Edna watched various emotions play across her son's face as he spoke of his wife and realized what a strong and responsible man this child of hers had become. She waited patiently for him to continue.

He smiled as he went on. "I don't know what she sees in me, but the more I got to know her, the more attracted I became until finally I wanted to be around her all the time. She's a good person and so interested in everything, and she's always wanted children, lots of children. I don't think Michele really thought about it one way or the other. To her, it was something young couples did. They had children." At that moment he must have seen the look of surprise on her face, because he put his hand out as if to steady her.

"Oh, I don't mean to say she didn't love Jillian. She did, and she was a good mother. I guess the difference is that Michele didn't want to stay home and be a full-time wife and mother, not like Karissa … or you," he finished with a weak grin. The look in his eyes pleaded with her to understand.

Edna couldn't help a small chuckle at what she took to be her son's belated attempt at flattery. "I think I know what you're trying to say." She reached across the small square table to pat his arm. "How long have you known Karissa?"

"About two years. She started working in the accounting department at Office Plus early last year. I enjoyed her company a lot, but I hadn't even thought about asking her out. Then, suddenly Michele was gone, and I was spending every non-working moment at home with Jillian. We were both trying to cope with the sudden loss." He drained his water glass and put it aside, running a finger in the ring of condensation it had left on the tabletop. After a moment of silence he sat back abruptly in his chair and said, "Actually, it was Anita who brought Karissa and me together eventually."

Edna was puzzled. "What do you mean?"

"Anita asked me to help her with the company's New Year's party. I wouldn't have gone, what with Michele's funeral only three weeks before, but Rice was called out of town unexpectedly and so was Marcie. Anita had already volunteered to organize the big company-sponsored event. She needed someone to help with the awards ceremony. Since several of the people in my department were receiving commendations, she asked me to fill in. The gala event was held downtown at the Convention Center." He waggled his eyebrows as if to let Edna know how impressive that was.

She didn't feel like smiling at his antics. She was still confused. "I thought Anita was Michele's best friend. Didn't she realize you'd still be mourning? Wasn't she mourning herself?"

Grant shrugged and went on, ignoring the questions. "Jillian was going to a friend's for a sleep-over, so Anita probably thought I shouldn't be alone on New Year's Eve. She's a big one for celebrating holidays, and I was still so numb, I didn't care what I did."

"I take it Karissa was also at the party."

"Yes, she was." His grin broadened as he studied the tabletop and lost himself for a minute in the memory. "She was beautiful. We danced a lot that night." Then he shook himself, as if suddenly aware he had been talking too much. "End of story, or the start of it, I guess you might say."

"What did Jillian think when you were married so soon after her mother died?"

"I wanted Jillian to have a mother." His eyes seemed to plead for understanding before he sat back again and explained further. "I couldn't take care of her by myself. Besides, she and Karissa hit it off right away. I don't think she minded at all having another female around."

Edna realized she was letting an opportunity slip by to find out more about the mystery woman. "And Anita? Was she pleased about the wedding, too?"

Grant lifted his arm, making a small production of looking at his watch. "Gosh, look at the time. I really should be getting back to the office."

He stood, picked up the debris from the table and headed toward a lidded trashcan near the front door. She hurried after him. The walk back to the office was silent, and she sensed a barrier had gone up between them again. *Why didn't he want to talk about Anita,* she wondered. Something had to be wrong.

As they approached the building, Grant said, "Would you like a tour of the place? I have some time to show you around, but it'll have to be quick."

"Yes, I'd like that." She had thought for a panicky moment that he might make an excuse and renege on his promise to show her the office. If he wouldn't talk to her about Anita, she needed to find someone who would. Just how she would go about it, she had no idea, but she hoped something would come to mind.

Grant opened the front door and she preceded him into the lobby, recognizing the person behind the desk as the gushing redhead to whom she had been introduced at the funeral the day before.

"Peter wants to see you," the woman said to Grant, handing him several pink message slips.

He turned to Edna, "Peter's head of our finance department. This shouldn't take long. You remember Brea, don't you?"

"Of course," Edna said, thankful to her son for reminding her of the young woman's name.

"Then, if you'll wait here, I'll be back shortly."

There were no inside doors visible to the room. Behind the receptionist's area stood a tall, curved partition with the company name and logo in big white letters against a bluish-gray background. It looked as though the ends of the partition, if moved forward, would form a giant oval with the edges of the reception counter. Grant walked around and disappeared behind the freestanding structure.

"Nice to see you again," Edna said, wondering how well Brea and Anita had known each other.

"Yeah," Brea replied. Pursing her lips into a pout that she apparently thought was becoming, she pulled at a strand of hair.

Edna speculated on how much time the young woman might spend making such short hair look so messy. She tried again to make pleasant chatter while she waited. "What a lovely big office you have." She gestured at the sun-lit lobby.

Brea frowned and gave a one-shoulder shrug. "This isn't my desk. The receptionist is late." She picked up a sheaf of papers and tamped them on the desk before wedging them into a blue file folder. "When I get my promotion, I won't be sitting out here at all." She gave Edna a self-satisfied smile. "Won't be long now, I can tell you that."

Only when Edna saw the woman sulk, did she remember that Brea had been introduced as Rice Ryan's secretary. Or was it administrative assistant? Realizing Brea needed little if any encouragement to talk, Edna prompted, "Oh? Congratulations. What will you be doing?"

Before Brea could answer, another young woman stepped out from behind the partition. She was plump with straight, shoulder-length brown hair and wore a tailored green shirt tucked into loose-fitting tan trousers. "Oh," she said, seeming startled. "Isn't Nina back yet?"

"Obviously not," Brea retorted, not looking at her co-worker.

"Well, I've got the new bus passes. She needs to have people sign for them. When will she be back?"

"You can leave them here. I'll see she gets your message." Brea's tone was haughty and she barely looked at the other woman as she patted the desk beside her.

The woman laid a large manila envelope on the edge of the desk and turned to disappear as quickly as she had arrived. As soon as her co-worker was out of sight, Brea snatched up the envelope, opened it and dumped several passes out onto the surface of the desk. Rummaging for a minute, she put one aside and returned the rest.

"How nice to be able to take a bus to work," Edna said, pretending not to notice that Brea hadn't signed the accompanying list. She didn't want to antagonize a possible source of information about Anita.

"Yeah, it's okay. I catch it in the morning, but Rice usually drives me home at night." She flicked her eyes toward Edna, seemingly to discover how she was responding to this news.

Edna, remembering that Rice was still married to Anita, merely said, "He sounds like a thoughtful boss."

Brea began to tap the eraser end of a pencil against the desk in a constant, monotonous rhythm. "Pretty much. We work late a lot. He's always driving me home. Says he doesn't want me falling asleep at the wheel." She gave Edna another sly glance from beneath half-closed eyelids. "My car was getting left here overnight a lot, so I told Rice he had to authorize a company bus pass for me." She shrugged, continuing to drum on the desk.

Nervous habit, Edna thought, and was wondering why Brea should be so jittery when another young woman appeared from behind the partition. Edna recognized the short black curls and lovely blue eyes of the receptionist Grant had been talking to when she'd first arrived.

"About time." Brea rose abruptly, tossing aside the pencil and picking up the blue folder.

"Three minutes late," the receptionist retorted, wrinkling her nose behind Brea's back.

"I have better things to do than sit here waiting for you to get back from lunch. Rice doesn't like my being away from my desk."

"Where is Rice today?"

Startled by a voice close behind her, Edna spun around to see another of the women she had been introduced to the day before, recognizing her as Marcie James, Anita's supervisor.

Brea responded with an air of importance. "He's out making a presentation to some new clients."

"I'll just bet," the woman mumbled so softly that Edna, standing beside her, was apparently the only one who had heard.

Marcie began leafing through a stack of pink message slips on the counter and spoke to Brea without looking at her. "Will he be around tomorrow? I need to see him about some accounts. I told him yesterday I wanted to meet with him."

"I'll let you know." Brea turned, chin jutting forward, and disappeared behind the partition.

Marcie, taking several of the messages and putting the rest back, spoke to the receptionist. "Will he be in the restaurant at the Omni tomorrow?"

Nina nodded. "Eleven to two, as usual. I haven't heard he won't be, and since I make all the out-of-town arrangements, I know he hasn't got a trip planned."

"Good. Maybe I'll catch him there. Now I know why he makes himself available off site. It's for those of us who can't get past his gatekeeper." She fluttered a hand in the direction Brea had just taken.

Both women laughed softly and Marcie turned, catching Edna's eye. She frowned a minute before brightening. "You're Grant's mother, aren't you? Edna."

"How nice of you to remember my name."

Marcie's smile brought a dimple to one cheek. "Actually, yours is easy for me. Edna was my grandmother's middle name. I like old-fashioned names." She looked around. "Does Grant know you're here?"

"Yes. We had lunch together." Glancing at her watch, she was surprised to see that she had been in the lobby for almost twenty minutes. "He had to see someone named Peter, then he was going to come right back and give me a tour of your offices."

"That would be Peter White, our CFO, Grant's boss." Marcie made a face. "If he's not back yet, he'll probably be a while." Pausing briefly, she looked at Edna as if making up her mind about something. Then she said as if on an impulse, "If you've got a minute, I'd like to speak with you."

Not quite believing her good fortune at this chance encounter with Anita's boss, Edna was quick to respond. "Certainly."

Marcie linked her arm through Edna's. "Come on, then. Why don't we go to my office? It's lots more comfortable than out here." Over her shoulder, she said, "Nina, when Grant gets back, tell him I've kidnapped his mother, will you, please?"

Eight

"I get the impression that Brea is very protective of Rice," Edna said, hoping to continue the gossipy mood. Smelling mint on Marcie's breath when she got closer, Edna wondered if the woman had had a sip or two of wine or something stronger with lunch. If so, perhaps she would be talkative.

"Thinks she's going to marry him, most likely. All his assistants have thought that," the blonde woman said, but Edna had no time to respond as she was led into a hallway behind the large partition. A corridor led off to both left and right, but the only doors visible were another double set of glass in front of them. Letting go of Edna's arm, the sales supervisor opened the right-hand panel and motioned Edna to precede her into a large room filled with computer desks and buzzing with the activity of ringing phones and conversations.

"These are our telemarketers." Marcie gestured at the room as she strode forward.

Except for a few curious looks as the two women walked by, most eyes stayed focused on the computer screens before them. Here and there a miniature stuffed animal or action figure sat atop a monitor, and several desks sported a plant or two, the only color in an otherwise brown and beige room. Marcie moved to an office at the end of the room, unlocked it and ushered Edna inside.

Speculating as to why Marcie might need to lock her door, she walked into the supervisor's office. One wall was almost floor-to-ceiling glass with a view of an inner courtyard. "What a lovely place to work," she exclaimed, crossing the room.

Water lilies floated in a round pool where a column of water shot up from the center. Droplets sparkled in the sunshine as gravity pulled the beads down again to splash the surface. She could see spots of color move about beneath the greenery and thought they must be the bright orange and yellow carp so popular in garden ponds these days.

"Thank you. I have to admit, the fountain is particularly soothing." Marcie tossed her handbag and keys on an armchair next to her desk and motioned to the leather sofa against the opposite wall. Striding to a credenza and picking up a thermal carafe, she raised it toward Edna questioningly. "Would you like a cup of coffee? Grant might be a while."

Edna was still inwardly marveling at her luck at having a private conversation with Anita's supervisor. Full from lunch, she wanted nothing else to put into her stomach. What she said aloud was, "That would be very nice. Thank you."

"I met your husband last week." Marcie came to sit on the sofa beside Edna, carefully putting cups and saucers on the low table before them.

"Oh? Was he here in the office?"

"Yes. Grant was showing him around, and I ran into them," Marcie grimaced, "literally. I was racing to my office to catch a call. Went dashing around that darned partition behind the reception desk and almost knocked

Albert onto his backside."

Edna laughed along with Marcie at the mental picture she had conjured up.

"Honestly, I keep telling them that wall is an accident waiting to happen, but it's supposed to be the latest thing in office décor." She shrugged. "Anyway, I just wanted to tell you I thought your husband was charming, such a gentleman."

"Why, thank you."

Marcie was looking at her from the corner of an eye as she sipped coffee, a look that made Edna realize Marcie hadn't invited her to the office solely for the seating comfort. Grant's co-worker had ulterior motives. Well, that was okay, so did Edna.

"How many people do you supervise?" she nodded toward the door to the telemarketing pool.

"Twenty inside sales staff, but I have another twelve out in the field." Marcie spoke proudly of her domain.

"Grant was telling me that Anita Collier is a member of your sales staff. That could be difficult, I imagine, having your boss's wife work for you." Edna hoped her comment sounded sympathetic.

"He might not be my boss much longer." Marcie reached to return her coffee cup to the table before settling back into the soft leather of the couch.

Here was a second subordinate of Rice Ryan's to hint at a change in the company. "Are you going to work for someone else?"

"I hope so." Marcie's smile didn't reach her eyes as she stretched an arm across the back of the sofa and half turned toward Edna. "Grant hasn't told you?" she asked after a brief pause during which she studied Edna's face.

"Tell me what?"

"The company is in a state of flux right now. Our CEO recently announced his retirement, and our board of directors is interviewing for his replacement. Rice is one of the applicants, but so are Peter White and two men from outside the company. If Rice doesn't get the job, I think he'll quit. If he does get it, I know I'll quit."

"I have an idea that would be a shame," Edna hurried to say. "I have the impression you know a great deal about the business. How long have you worked for Office Plus?"

Marcie seemed to perk up at the compliment. "Sixteen years next month."

"Did you start as a telemarketer? Is that the natural progression?"

"Typically, but no. I started as Rice's secretary. That's what the position was called back then, and that's when he was Director of Operations."

"Oh. I don't know why, but I had the idea he hadn't been that long with the company?"

"Sixteen years, same as me. I interviewed for the secretarial position right after Office Plus hired him away from some company in Chicago. I thought I'd died and gone to heaven when he offered me the job. Guess I was bowled over by his charm and good looks." She made a face. "How stupid we can be when we're young."

Remembering Marcie's comment about Rice's assistants, Edna said, "Are you one of the secretaries he was going to marry?"

"Sure am." Frowning, Marcie leaned forward to pick up her cup and take a sip of coffee, not meeting Edna's eyes. "But that's old news."

"Do you mind my asking what happened?"

She surprised herself, asking such a personal question of someone she'd just met. At first she didn't think Marcie was going to answer, but after several moments of fiddling with her cup and saucer, the other woman sat back. "The man can't keep his eyes or hands at home. Every woman he meets seems to be a challenge until he gets her into bed. Then it's 'Good-bye, Sweetie. Don't let the door hit ya on the way out.'"

"He's like that with everybody?" She was thinking of Anita, the one woman he'd finally married.

"Rice uses people. He's a manipulator. One minute, you think you're the only one he cares about, and then wham! It's over, and you never knew what hit you." She bent forward, elbows resting on her knees, studying her fingertips. Marcie seemed to be looking into the past, speaking more to herself than to Edna. "If you ask me, the only thing that man cares about is money. It's for sure he has no respect for women."

"I've had friends tell me similar stories about men they've known. What makes them flit from woman to woman like that, do you suppose?"

"I don't know. What I do know about Rice is that he grew up in a poor neighborhood in Chicago. Now that he has money and a certain amount of power with his position in the company, he likes to strut. I think a woman to him is just something pretty to dangle on his arm. Like I said, he sees a pretty face and he's got to have it, but once he's conquered her, she doesn't mean a thing anymore."

Edna tucked the information about Rice's background away in her head to tell Ernie when she saw him next. To Marcie, she said, "But he married Anita. Sounds like he changed, at least for a little while." She wondered if perhaps Marcie was jealous and angry that she hadn't been Rice's choice for a wife. Unbidden, a new thought popped into her mind and she wondered if Rice knew about the money Anita's father, and now Anita herself, would inherit. As soon as the idea entered her head, Edna dismissed it. How could he possibly know when Anita herself didn't?

"Yeah, go figure," Marcie said, breaking into Edna's thoughts. "I'd have bet that if the time ever came for Rice to settle down, he'd have married for money or social position, at least. Anita makes a good salary but not as good as mine. Her parents didn't leave much of an estate, and although they were well-known and terrific people, they weren't members of Denver's elite, not by a long shot." She hesitated before adding, "I find it hard to believe, though, that it was love. The only person Rice has ever loved is himself."

"If you're right, he's probably a very lonely person," Edna said, uncertain how to reply to this woman who obviously had been deeply hurt by Rice Ryan. She wondered that Marcie seemed to harbor so much resentment for the man, yet still worked for him. But she wanted to talk about Anita and the present, not about Marcie's past. "I understand the marriage hasn't lasted very long. Grant says Anita's going to file for divorce."

Marcie's frown deepened. "I hadn't heard that. According to Rice, Anita's been upset over losing her parents so suddenly, but she and Rice are getting back together. As a matter of fact, I think he's trying to force me out so he can give her my job." She snorted. "First, he sets her up in a territory that insures she'll be out of town most of the time, probably to make it easier for him to cheat on her, and now, he wants her in the office. He won't have nearly the freedom he's used to." Her laugh held no amusement before she said, "I wonder how Brea's going to feel about that."

Edna spoke her next thoughts aloud. "The CEO of a large company would have social obligations, I'd imagine. Perhaps Rice realizes he needs his wife around if he's to be a leader in the community. A divorce could hurt him, maybe even ruin his chances of getting the promotion."

Marcie stared at her as if the idea came as a surprise. "That's right. He hasn't gotten the job yet, by God." Then, her look softened as she straightened up and leaned slightly toward Edna in a conspiratorial pose. "Look, Edna, since Grant apparently hasn't had time to discuss all this with you, I'll fill you in on what's about to happen." Edna raised an eyebrow in question but didn't respond, so Marcie went on. "As part of the search process for the new CEO, all of us mid-level managers in the company have been asked to give our input. As a group we'll have a chance next week to talk to each of the candidates and give our impressions to the board."

Edna pulled back slightly to get a better look into Marcie's eyes, trying to gauge her intentions. "It sounds like a good idea. Is that a common practice for businesses?"

Marcie scoffed. "Not hardly. I think Steve, our outgoing president, suggested it, and the board is going along to please him. I have a feeling Rice has convinced Steve that most of the employees support him. Support Rice, that is."

"And you don't think that's the case." She made it a statement rather than a question as she noticed the disgust on Marcie's face.

"I think he's on a campaign to get internal votes. He wouldn't dare approach me. He already knows how I feel. I have wondered, though, if he's been talking to Grant." At this, she looked meaningfully at Edna.

"Grant hasn't mentioned any of this to me, but I haven't gotten the impression that he is particularly fond of Rice. If I had to guess, I'd say Grant resents the way Rice has treated Anita." Edna tried to draw Marcie's attention back to her particular interest, but the woman seemed intent on her own agenda.

"I bet anything Rice is dangling the directorship of the computer department under Grant's nose." Marcie gave another sneer. "He'll promise the world, but he'll never deliver. I know that from personal experience."

"Have you told Grant what you're telling me?"

"I've tried, but I don't think he believes me. He probably thinks it's sour grapes coming from me."

Edna thought for a minute. "How does Anita feel about Rice becoming CEO? I mean, has she spoken to you about it?"

"This has all come about only in the last few weeks. I haven't talked to Anita since her parents' funeral."

This last bit was something Edna had hoped to find out and she felt excitement quicken her heartbeat. Outwardly, however, she frowned, feigning confusion. "But I thought she worked for you."

Surprisingly, Marcie smiled and seemed to relax, laying aside her fight with Rice for the moment. She was obviously on more comfortable ground when it came to the details of her job. "I'm not the type of manager who hovers. My people know what I expect of them and they do it or they move on to another company. Simple as that."

Edna was taken aback at the callousness with which Marcie could dismiss another person's livelihood. "It's one thing not to hover, but I would think you would have to be in contact your sales people on a regular basis. Have you heard from her at all?"

"At her parents' funeral, I told her to take some time off. After that, I assume she went back to work. I admit, though, I am surprised she didn't show up for Lia's service." Marcie shrugged. "But then, she may have felt she couldn't handle another funeral so soon after her parents'."

"So you aren't concerned that you haven't heard from her?"

"Not particularly. It's not unusual. I don't have much contact with my field personnel unless their sales are down. That definitely isn't the case with Anita."

"She never calls in to the office?"

"Not unless there's a problem."

"What about actual sales? I don't know much about how businesses operate, but doesn't she have to let someone in the office know if she makes a new sale or something?" She thought Anita would have to have spoken to somebody in the office during the last several weeks.

Marcie laughed. "You should ask Grant about that. He's done a great job of automating the process for us. Everyone in the field carries a laptop computer. Sales are recorded and downloaded to our main database. We receive orders all day long. Grant has two full-time people who monitor the orders and another to make sure our communication lines stay up."

Edna shook her head. "I'm afraid this is way over my head."

Marcie was obviously pleased to explain. "All our customers have standing orders. They're what we call blanket orders that are filled on a regular basis. Nobody has to contact this office unless they want to change an order. Most of our customers log in themselves to make any necessary revision before the next consignment is scheduled to ship. It's all done over the Internet."

Edna was still skeptical about the personnel issues. "How do you know if someone is still working for you? How do you know they haven't quit and gone to work for another company?"

Marcie yielded slightly. "Actually, I usually do hear at least once a week from most of my people when they're in the field. In any case, I have a mandatory monthly staff meeting. As a matter of fact, there's one scheduled for next Friday, a week from today. Anita will show up for that. If not, she's got to call in and give me a darn good reason why she won't be here."

Edna did a quick mental calculation. "If you haven't seen her since the funeral, she must have missed the last meeting."

"That was shortly after I told her to take some time off. I didn't expect her to attend last month. As I said, her sales have been outstanding this year, so I wasn't concerned when she didn't show up or call in. I doubt she'll skip another, though. If I do say so, the meetings are very informative and inspiring."

Edna felt as if a weight had been lifted from her shoulders. Why hadn't anyone told her this before? Anita would be here next Friday. Certainly, Grant should have known. Why hadn't he simply told this to Ernie? Thinking of the detective, she felt elated over the good news she would have for him. At most, Ernie would have only six more days to wait before he could speak to Anita.

Looking at her watch, she was surprised to see it was nearly two-thirty. She had to be back at the house by three o'clock when Jillian got home. She was about to say as much to Marcie when a knock sounded on the door and Grant poked his head in.

"Sorry I got waylaid."

Marcie waved a hand for him to enter. "That's okay. Your mother and I had a great chat, didn't we, Edna?"

Edna smiled, rose from the couch and extended her hand to the other woman. "A very nice visit. Thank you, Marcie."

Grant escorted Edna out of the building, apologizing that he hadn't gotten away from Peter in time to give her a tour of the plant.

"Marcie was telling me about Rice and Peter vying for the CEO position," she said as they headed toward the visitors' parking area. "Which one do you hope will get the job?"

"I get along okay with both of them," Grant said, noncommittally, as he shoved his hands into his pants pockets and walked with his head down. After a slight pause, he added, "I imagine she gave you an earful about Rice."

"As a matter of fact, she did. She says her days will be numbered if Rice is chosen to head the company."

"She probably doesn't really care who gets it. According to the grape vine, Marcie's already job hunting. I don't think it will take her long to find something else.

She's good at what she does. Too bad she got involved with Rice back when. She's blamed him for her lack of promotions ever since, but I think it's her attitude that's done most of the damage. Maybe it'll be good for her to move on." They'd arrived at the car by that time, and he opened the door for her before turning hurriedly to stride back to the building.

Leaving the parking lot, she stopped for a car that was pulling out of a space farther down the row. Driving by the newly emptied slot, she noticed a shiny black coupe with darkly tinted windows driving down the next lane, parallel to her. It looked exactly like the one she had seen in Grant's neighborhood yesterday.

She was puzzling over the coincidence when the blast of a horn startled her attention back to her own driving where she was drifting to the left, heading toward another vehicle that was approaching the visitors' parking area. She swerved back to avoid a head-on collision and, heart pounding, managed to exit the lot without further incident and without spotting the black car again.

On the way home, she glanced several times in the rearview mirror, wondering if she was being followed. *Ridiculous*, she thought with a shake of her head. *Why would anyone be tailing me?* "I must stop being so paranoid," she muttered, as her eyes strayed once more to the rearview mirror.

Nine

Arriving at the house, Edna pulled into the garage, as she and Grant had discussed. The Celica had no air conditioning, and Grant said the car would be like an oven if it sat in the Colorado sun, regardless of how cool the air temperature was outside. She pressed the remote that was clipped to the sun visor. As the garage door buzzed and clanked its descent, she turned and pushed herself out of the driver's seat. When she did so, she glanced backward in time to see the lower half of a shiny black coupe moving slowly past the house. She bent, hoping to catch sight of the driver, but the garage door dropped too quickly.

Was it the same car? There must be more than one new-looking black vehicle in the area. She suddenly thought of Jillian. What if the car belonged to a child molester? What if he was casing the neighborhood, waiting for a chance to grab some unsuspecting youngster? If it was the same car she had seen in the neighborhood yesterday, what was it doing at Grant's office today? She must try to get the license plate number. Maybe Ernie could get the owner's name for her.

Hurrying into the house and over to the wide living room window, she parted the filmy white curtains to look into the street. No black car in sight. As a matter of fact, there were no cars on the street at all, parked or moving. She turned and strode down the hall, hearing voices and laughter before she reached Karissa's bedroom door.

Entering the room, she saw her daughter-in-law lying in her usual position on her left side, surrounded by pillows. This afternoon the rest of the bed was almost completely covered with magazines. A woman she hadn't met before was sitting on a chair beside the bed. The two women were flipping through the publications, showing each other different pages and chattering away like a couple of magpies.

"Edna, you're home." Karissa, looking up from an issue of *Oprah*, sounded happy to see her. "Come meet my friend Sudie."

The stout woman, her dark hair woven into a single long braid that hung down her back, smiled and nodded, trying to stand as she clutched at a small stack of magazines in her lap. "I'm happy to meet you."

"Please don't get up. It's nice to meet you, too." Edna nodded her acknowledgment of the introduction before turning to Karissa. "Where's Jillian? Is she home from school?"

Her daughter-in-law frowned. "She's spending the afternoon at a friend's. Hallie's mom called to ask if it was okay. Why? Is something wrong? You look worried."

"I just saw a black car drive by. I saw the same one yesterday. At least, it looked like the same one." Listening to her own words, she realized again she might be mistaken about the car. She knew nothing about automobiles except that the one she had seen on both occasions was small, sporty looking, and seemed well cared for. "Do you know if anyone around here drives a shiny black car with tinted windows?"

Sudie and Karissa looked at each other as if communicating by mental telepathy. After a few faint facial and shoulder gestures, they both turned back to her. "No," Sudie said with an accent so slight Edna wondered if she had imagined it. "I live across the street, two houses down." She waved vaguely to her left. "The car you describe doesn't sound like one I've seen around."

"Didn't Tio get home from the service a few days ago?" Karissa asked Sudie.

"He was supposed to, but I haven't seen him yet." She turned to Edna, explaining, "Antonio's my next door neighbor's boy. Karissa's right. It might be his car. I'll call over there tonight and ask them just to be sure."

Feeling only slightly better, she left the two women to their magazines and went to change into slacks and a pullover. Having the afternoon unexpectedly to herself, she felt at loose ends. She wanted to talk to Ernie, tell him what she had learned about Anita, but she had no way of contacting him. Thinking of Anita reminded her that she wanted to browse back issues of the local newspapers to see what she could find out about the Colliers' accident.

Edna let Karissa know where she was going and set off on foot. She didn't see a black car but kept an eye out for one as she walked six blocks to the library. She and Albert had discovered the place on one of their jaunts around the area, and she had been meaning to go back, delighted to know it was so close.

Inside the small, single-story brick building, Edna quickly found the newspaper and magazine racks. She selected several back issues of the *Arvada Sentinel* and took them to a nearby table. The article she was looking for was in the third issue she perused, six weeks back, under the headline "Couple Killed in Auto Crash." The short piece barely described the accident, saying only that the brakes had failed as the car descended the hill at Sixty-Ninth and Ward Road. One witness, a man who had been about to cross at the walk located north of the accident site, saw the car descending much too fast before it veered out of control. The car jumped the curb and sideswiped a lamp post before rolling onto its top and coming to rest against a wooden fence. From other reports, police believed Collier swerved to avoid a cat, which probably caused him to lose control of the vehicle. Both Harrington Collier and his wife Loretta were pronounced dead at the scene.

After reading the article Edna sat staring down at the newsprint, thinking how quickly one's life could change. She folded the papers and returned them to the racks, sad and depressed. As she walked home, she wondered what it must feel like for a young woman to lose both parents in such a senseless manner. Two fatal accidents. No, three, she thought, remembering Michele's disaster last winter. Anita had recently lost not only her parents but two close friends.

Sudie was gone by the time Edna got back to the house. Karissa was lying on the couch in the living room with several throw pillows supporting her shoulders and head. After hanging up her coat and hat, Edna stood before the entryway mirror to fluff her curls back into place, noticing as she did so the sadness in her eyes. She made a determined effort to look more cheerful than she felt as she went to sit near Karissa. Her daughter-in-law was leafing through an issue of *Sewing World*.

Grabbing onto the topic as a distraction from her dismal thoughts, she said, "Do you sew?"

"Yes. I make all my clothes. Jillian's too," Karissa added, smiling shyly.

Thinking back to some of the outfits she had seen on her granddaughter, Edna's eyes widened in amazement. "Even her jerseys and slacks?"

"Yes, everything. I made her a down parka last winter."

Before this, she had thought Karissa a spendthrift with all her talk about shopping and her constant leafing through magazines. Now she realized her daughter-in-law must be gathering ideas for styles. She was trying to adjust to this new mental image of Karissa when Jillian burst through the front door.

"I'm home," the youngster shouted to the room, tossing a small red backpack at the closet door and heading into the living room.

Edna's heart warmed at the sight of the child, although she mentally shook her head at the careless way Jillian discarded her belongings.

Karissa laughed and shouted back without sitting up, "Hi, Jilly. Glad you're home." Then, in a more subdued voice, she said, "Did I just hear a backpack hit the floor?"

Apparently Jillian had been reprimanded before because without losing a step, she spun around and headed back to the entryway. "Yes, Ma'am. I'm sorry." She picked up her pack, opened the closet and hung it on one of several low hooks that had obviously been installed for her on the back of the door.

Edna watched in amusement as Jillian flounced over to give her grandmother a hug before bestowing a quick kiss on Karissa's cheek. She then lifted the magazine to see what her stepmother was reading.

"You miss making things, don't you?" she said, perching on the edge of the sofa as Karissa shifted her weight to make some room for the little girl.

"Yes, Sweetie, I do." She tickled Jillian as she replied, then added, "Your father called to say he has to work late again tonight."

Jillian's face fell. "Again," she wailed.

Ignoring the child's reaction, Karissa said, "What are you going to make your grandmother and me for dinner?"

Jillian's enthusiasm returned as quickly as it had disappeared. She jumped up from the sofa yelling, "Tacos."

"Quietly, child. We're right here beside you. No need to shout." Karissa put her hands over her ears, a mock look of pain on her face. "Why don't you show your grandmother how to make them? Can you do that?"

"Yes." Jillian's excitement was apparent, but she kept her voice down. "Want to, Gramma?"

"That sounds like fun."

Edna, impressed with Karissa's easy way with Jillian, followed her granddaughter to the kitchen, leaving Karissa to her magazines. She was slowly developing a more complete picture of Grant's second wife, and she liked what she saw.

For the next half hour she and Jillian browned and drained hamburger meat and chopped tomatoes and lettuce. Jillian insisted on grating the cheese, which was fine with Edna. When it came time to make guacamole, Jillian had to run into the living room several times to confer with her stepmother, but eventually all ingredients were on the table along with place settings and Karissa waddled into the dining room to eat. The plates with their red, green and yellow ingredients looked festive.

Both Jillian and Karissa laughed watching Edna follow

their instructions for making a taco and then trying to eat it without dumping the filling out the opposite end. She had finally gotten the hang of it and taken her first successful bite, savoring the spicy taste, so different from what she was used to, when the cell phone in her pocket went off. Excusing herself, she left the table and went into the next room to answer the call. Typically, she would have left it unanswered and picked up her message after dinner, but she had missed Albert's calls too often recently. As it turned out, it wasn't her husband but Ernie who was calling.

"I'm at Safeway," he said, without preamble.

"And I'm in the middle of dinner. Can I call you back?" Edna kept her tone low, not wanting Karissa to hear.

"When can you get here?"

Edna looked at the clock on the mantelpiece. It was a few minutes past six. "I'll meet you there at eight." She pressed the disconnect button after hearing Ernie grumble an impatient, "Okay."

She pocketed her phone and, with a murmur of apology to Karissa and Jillian as she returned to the table, looked down at her partly-eaten taco. Bravely, she picked up the brittle tortilla shell and wedged the hamburger and toppings back into place with her fork before taking another bite. "Mmm," she rolled her eyes at her granddaughter, making the child giggle with delight.

Later that evening, after settling Jillian into bed and telling Karissa that she wanted to pick up a few things at the store, she backed the Celica out of the garage and headed for the Safeway shopping center. She found Ernie at the same small table near the deli counter.

"What did you find out?" he asked, helping her off with her coat and presenting her with a lukewarm cup of coffee.

Pushing aside the Styrofoam cup, she leaned forward, bursting with her good news. "Anita will be in town next Friday, a week from tomorrow."

Ernie's reaction wasn't what she expected. Throwing back his head with a look of anguish, he slammed a fist into the palm of his other hand. "That might be too late. The doctors say it'll be a miracle if Mrs. Maitland lasts through the weekend."

Edna felt both surprise and dismay. "How do you know that?"

"My client. He says she probably won't even last that long. We've got to find her niece." Ernie looked away momentarily before turning to ask, "Did you find anyone at all who has talked to Anita since her parents' funeral?"

"No one."

"Anyone who might know how to reach her or where she might have gone?"

Again, Edna shook her head. She thought back to her conversation with Marcie. "Her supervisor thinks she's working somewhere in her territory. Grant's pretty sure she's gone off to be alone for a while. None of her friends or coworkers has seen or heard from her in the last five weeks, and although she's not been out of touch for this long a time before, nobody seems to be at all worried except for my son. I'm beginning to believe you're right. I think something has happened to her."

"Isn't there anything you learned that might help track her down?" As he spoke, Ernie took the small notebook and pen out of his inside jacket pocket. "Did her supervisor mention a client's name? What about a favorite place? Has Grant said anything about where Anita goes when she wants to be alone?"

"No." Edna shook her head. Disappointed at his reaction to what she'd thought would be good news, she forced her mind back over everything she had heard or seen that day. For a moment she thought of telling him about the black car but then decided not to. She would wait to hear from Sudie if it belonged to the boy next door. Feeling as though she had failed Ernie, she said, "What did you discover today?"

The detective turned a few pages in his notebook and studied his scribbles. "I talked to a guy I know works ski patrol during the winter, up where your daughter-in-law had her accident. He wasn't on the slope when it happened, but he knows someone who was. He said he'd talk to the kid and get back to me." Ernie turned to the next page and read more of the hen-scratches before returning the notebook to his pocket. Apparently, there was nothing else he had to report.

The two sat in silence for a while, each with his or her own thoughts. She took a sip from the Styrofoam cup, but the liquid had turned cold and bitter. "Where do we go from here?" she asked, certain they had reached a dead end.

He shrugged, turning his face so he looked at her from the corner of his eye. "I'd still like to talk to your son."

She didn't speak for several heartbeats. She knew she couldn't ask Grant to speak to Ernie. Instead, she changed the subject. "Will you show me where Anita lives? I think I can get away for a few hours tomorrow, and I'd like to see her place." She didn't know why, but at that moment she felt the need to see not only Anita's home, but also her parents' house. It was something physical she could do, something other than sitting around doing nothing and getting nowhere.

Before he could answer, the cell phone in her tote began to jingle. Two women came into the deli area, chatting noisily, at the same time Edna spoke into the phone.

"Sounds like you're out on the town again." Albert's voice was faint.

Holding a finger to one ear, she pressed the mobile harder into the other. "I can barely hear. Is that you, Albert?"

"Were you expecting someone else?"

She heard him more clearly this time and was annoyed at the question. "It might have been Karissa or Grant calling."

"Where are you? Aren't you with them?"

"No. I'm at the grocery store." Probably because she was depressed at getting nowhere in the search for Anita, Edna felt herself growing irritated at Albert's interrogation. If he was so concerned about where she was or who she was with, why hadn't he stayed in Colorado? "Let me call you back when I've finished shopping." She disconnected the call without waiting for his reply.

Ten

Grant was sitting at the kitchen counter when Edna walked in from the garage.

"Where have you been?" He sounded like his father.

Still irritated at Albert's implied suspicions, she did not trust herself to answer cheerfully. Instead, she held up a grocery bag containing the quart of milk and several apples she had bought before leaving the store. Before he spoke again, she turned her back to put her purchases into the refrigerator and get control of her temper.

"I got home right after you left." He was looking at the kitchen wall clock when she spun back to face him. "You've been gone over an hour."

"I wanted some time to myself," she replied noncommittally. Her annoyance was growing over his questioning her, but at the same time guilt gnawed her conscience over having done something he'd specifically asked her not to do.

He must have seen a spark in her eyes because he said hastily, "I thought you'd be here taking care of Karissa and Jillian when I got home." He paused, frowning for a second. "Jillian said you promised her a kitten. What's that all about?"

Edna began to unbutton her overcoat, still not fully in control of her temper. By the time she had removed the garment, she'd reassessed the situation. It wasn't typical of her son to lash out at her, particularly with absurd accusations. When she spoke, her tone was soft and calmer than she felt. "Karissa knew where I was and knows how to reach me if she needs to, and you know I wouldn't promise Jillian any such thing without your approval first. What's really bothering you, Grant?"

He backed down. She seemed to have knocked the wind out of his sails. "I'm sorry, Ma, but I started to worry about you when you were gone so long."

"I've been out of the house barely an hour. I don't think that's what's troubling you."

His gaze dropped to the newspaper spread before him on the counter, but she doubted he was reading. Maybe if she opened up to him, she could shake loose whatever was on his mind. She draped her coat over an arm and clutched it to her middle before beginning to speak. "Actually, I ran into Ernie, the detective, at the store." She didn't explain that it had been a prearranged appointment. Let him assume what he would. When he raised his head, she saw anger begin to spread across his face. She hurried on before he could explode. "Why won't you talk to him? He's not going away, you know. Won't it be best if you simply tell him what you know?"

Grant stood and came around the counter. "I guess we'd better talk, Mother." Taking her coat and with a gentle hand on her elbow, he steered her toward the living room. Draping the coat on a nearby chair, he motioned her to the sofa before taking the corner opposite her and resting an arm across the back as he turned to look at her.

"Apparently, I can't stop you from talking to Ernie Freedman, so I'm going to tell you what I know. You can decide if you should tell him or not, but I'm hoping you'll keep this to yourself."

She nodded and waited for him to go on.

After a few seconds' pause, as if giving his mother a chance to say something, he continued. "Anita was supposed to come here for dinner the day after her parents' funeral. Instead, when Karissa and I got home from a doctor's appointment, there was a message on the answering machine." He turned and leaned forward to rest his elbows on his knees, clasping his hands together. "She said she was going away and would call when she could. She asked that we not mention anything to anyone—and she emphasized *anyone*—about the call. Karissa was having one of her bad days and had gone to lie down. Anita sounded scared. I didn't want to upset my wife, so I erased the message and told her only that Anita had decided to go away for a few days."

"Anita didn't say where she was going or explain why she didn't want anyone to know?"

He sighed and swiveled his head to look over at her. "To be honest, I didn't hear everything she said. She must have been in her car, not at her house, and she was probably heading into the mountains because the call kept breaking up. I had to listen to the recording several times to understand the little I just told you."

"Don't you want to know where she is?"

"Of course I do." He ran both hands through his curly hair in a gesture of frustration as he straightened up. "Look, Ma, Anita was a bundle of nerves the last time I saw her. Her parents had just been killed in a freak accident, her marriage was on the rocks, and Rice was hassling her about the divorce."

She was surprised at this last statement. "Does Rice want a divorce so he can marry Brea?" When she thought about it, she didn't feel Brea would be the type of wife a young, ambitious executive would pick. She thought Brea was too immature and self-centered to put a husband's career first. A woman like that was more likely to put his charge cards first. Edna's mind returned to matters at hand when she heard Grant's short, mirthless laugh.

"No, just the opposite. Rice has been trying to persuade Anita to drop the idea. Now that she's the one who wants out of the marriage, he's changed his tune. Guess he's as close to groveling as that ego of his will allow."

"Aren't you concerned that you haven't heard anything from her in all this time?"

"Of course I am." He looked at her as if surprised she needed to ask. "But she said she wanted to be alone. No matter how worried I might be, I have to respect that. She's smart. She can take care of herself. For heaven's sake, she drives around that desolate territory of hers for weeks at a time."

Wondering if he was trying to convince himself as well as her, Edna reached out to touch his shoulder. Remembering what Ernie had said about a feeling of illusion, that Anita was there, but yet she wasn't there, she said, "If the message she left was so indistinct, are you certain it was Anita? Could it have been someone pretending to be her?"

He frowned. "Why would someone pretend to be her?" Picking up the remote control for the television, he sat back and frowned at her. "Don't go getting weird on me, Ma. I've told you what I know. She asked me to keep a confidence, telling me she needed to be alone for a while. Now, I'm asking you to respect *my* confidence." As if to signal the end of the conversation, he turned the set to the ten o'clock news as he added, "Besides, there really isn't anything to tell."

Edna caught very little of what the TV anchors had to say for the next twenty minutes or so. She was going over in her mind what Ernie had told her and what Grant had just said. She felt more than ever that something must have happened to Anita and snapped out of her reverie only when Grant turned off the television and the room went suddenly silent.

"I really wish you'd speak to Ernie." She tried once more to reason with her son, wanting to provoke some urgency in him. "You consider her a friend, and there's a possibility that she might be in serious trouble. Ernie's a professional. What in her message can't you tell anyone? You don't even know where she's gone, do you? Why don't you want to help? Working together, you and he may be able to find her."

With a deep sigh, Grant rose from his seat. "Ma, you haven't been listening to me. What if he's working for Rice? I won't betray her to a guy like that." He bent to kiss her cheek. "I know you're concerned, but she'll show up. You'll see. Now, I've had a long day and I've really got to get some sleep."

"Is it possible that Lia was killed because she knew Anita's whereabouts?"

He didn't react with the scorn she half expected. She had said it mostly to jar him out of a complacency she found both annoying and distressing. How could she instill in him some of her growing concern for Anita?

"You know, that's something that has never made sense to me. Lia didn't usually jog at that hour. Anita was the one who got up before dawn and ran before work, not Lia." He had picked up the TV's remote control and fiddled with it for several seconds before his next question took her off guard. "Did Freedman ever tell you why he's so intent on finding Anita?"

Hopeful that the question meant Grant might be willing to confide in Ernie, she told him about Anita's great-aunt and the inheritance that would be lost if an immediate relative didn't visit Elizabeth Maitland before the old woman died.

By the time she reached the end of her story, he had sat back down, and his expression showed alarm. "Ma, Anita doesn't have any relatives." He probably saw the doubt on her face because he grew more agitated. "When Michele talked so much about our families, Anita used to say she wished she'd had a brother or sister, or even an aunt or uncle. If this Freedman guy is handing you some cock-and-bull story about a dying great-aunt, he's a phony. I'm worried about you, Ma. I wish you'd listen to me and stay away from him."

"It's possible she might not have known about her great-aunt. Maybe her father never talked about his relatives from New York, since he'd had the falling out with his father."

Shaking his head, Grant placed the remote control on the coffee table and turned to take her hands in his. "What do you actually know about this guy? Even if we leave Rice out of the picture, you don't know really why Freedman is looking for her, do you? All you know is what he chooses to tell you, and it doesn't fit with what I know about Anita. Why are you willing to believe him and not me?"

His question took her by surprise. She didn't have an answer. She only felt she could trust Ernie and that someone needed to find Anita. Why would he make up such an elaborate lie if he wasn't who he claimed to be? Yet, Grant had a point. What did she know about the man?

Grant let go of her hands, finally breaking the growing silence. "I need to get to bed. I wish you'd think about what you're doing. And please, whatever you do, don't mention any of this to Karissa. I don't want her worrying about Anita on top of everything else she's going through."

Edna felt the unspoken condemnation in his voice, that he was afraid she, his mother, would endanger not only his wife but his unborn child. As she watched him retreat down the hall, she felt that any progress she had made that day to ease tensions with her son had been wiped away. She felt guilty about burdening him when his nerves must be on edge with the stress of his wife's condition on top of the long hours he'd been working. She thought about the phone message Anita had left and wasn't reassured that all was well.

Wearily, she got ready for bed, a sense of unease knotting her stomach. Just before she dropped off to sleep, she remembered she hadn't returned Albert's phone call.

Eleven

Next morning, Edna was startled awake by a loud knocking.

"Gramma, Gramma." Jillian's voice came through the door before the girl did. "Are you still sleeping?" She was standing by the bedside. "Daddy wants to know if you can drive me to school." She put a hand on Edna's shoulder and bent over to peer into her face.

Edna struggled to wake fully. "Yes. What time is it?" But Jillian had already run from the room and was shouting as she disappeared down the hall.

"She said yes, Daddy. Gramma will take me to school."

By the time Edna was dressed and in the kitchen, Grant had already made breakfast for his family and left for work, so she had no idea what sort of mood he was in. Jillian was sitting at the dining room table, finishing a bowl of cereal.

Karissa sat across from Jillian with a half-eaten breakfast of scrambled eggs and toast. She looked up as Edna came into the room. "The coffee's hot."

Edna was pouring the steaming liquid into a large ceramic mug when she remembered again that she had not yet called Albert. Excusing herself, she took her coffee into the living room, dug the cell phone out of her tote and pressed the speed dial number for her home in Rhode Island. After four rings the answering machine kicked in. Looking at the clock on the mantel, she figured it was about ten minutes past nine on the East Coast. If he was out of the house this early, Albert had probably gone to play golf. She left a message that she had called and was sorry to have missed him, before returning to the dining room as Jillian ran off to get her book bag.

"Sudie is coming to spend the day with me," Karissa said. "You're welcome to join us, but it's supposed to be another beautiful day. Sunny and low seventies. I know you probably miss your walks. I can give you directions to a couple of scenic hiking trails nearby, if you'd prefer to get outdoors for a bit."

"That's very thoughtful of you." Edna felt relief. She hadn't known how she would manage to leave the house long enough to visit the Colliers' residences. Karissa certainly made things easy for her. It was as if her daughter-in-law could read her mind. "Have you and Sudie made special plans for today?" she asked over the rim of her cup.

Karissa laughed, sounding happier than Edna had heard her recently. "Yes, we have. I'm teaching her how to do smocking. She wants to make a dress for her niece from a pattern I designed for Jilly."

As if on cue, Sudie came into the room carrying a large canvas bag and followed by a bouncing Jillian, who apparently had seen the neighbor and let her in before she had a chance to ring the doorbell. The women spent several minutes in pleasant conversation over their coffee before Jillian informed her grandmother it was time to leave for school.

After dropping Jilly at the elementary school, Edna drove to Safeway and went to the lunch area to wait for Ernie. She could have spent the half hour back at the house, but she wanted time to organize her thoughts. She had already decided to trust her intuition about the detective and ignore Grant's warnings. Besides, she would be sticking close to Ernie and once they found Anita, if he turned out to be something other than what he claimed … well, she would deal with that when the time came.

Buying coffee and a Danish, she took a table close to the wall and dug in her tote bag for paper and pencil, preparing to make a list of what she had learned about Anita so far. She had just bitten into the sticky, apple-cinnamon pastry when Ernie appeared at her shoulder, towering over her in his rumpled brown suit.

"You're early," he said.

"So are you," she replied after swallowing quickly and glancing at her watch.

"Thought I'd get here ahead of schedule and have breakfast. That looks good." He eyed her pastry.

She laughed at his hungry look, like a small child drooling over candy. "Go get yourself some breakfast. We're in no hurry. I have the next several hours off." She felt as though she were playing hooky from school.

By the time Ernie returned, she was still no closer to putting anything on paper. He had bought two glazed doughnuts and a large cup of coffee. He dropped several napkins down with the rest of his purchases as he squeezed his bulk into the chair opposite her.

She frowned, watching him take a big bite of doughnut. "None of this is making sense to me."

With his mouth full and unable to answer, he simply raised his eyebrows in question.

"Where do you suppose Anita could have gone, and why hasn't she called any of her friends or her workplace?

It's been about six weeks now, hasn't it?"

Ernie took a sip of coffee to wash down the doughnut. When he could talk, he said, "That's what I've been asking for the past four days." The twinkle in his eyes softened the what-do-you-think-I've-been-doing-all-this-time tone in his voice. "I've checked the hospitals and the morgue. I've contacted police and rescue departments, asking if there have been any accidents involving females matching Anita's description. She's been gone long enough that I'd expect more of a paper trail, but there isn't even that to go on."

"Paper trail?" she asked, jotting the words in her small notepad.

"Credit card receipts mostly. You know, from buying gas or staying in a motel. I can't believe the slips wouldn't have started coming in yet, but the credit companies don't have charges for any of her cards."

"How do you know?"

"Friend of a friend," he responded, taking another bite of doughnut and not looking at her.

She thought about that and decided not to ask him if it was legal to obtain such information. Instead, she said, "Could she be staying with someone? Maybe she has a cabin somewhere. Grant tells me that's a popular thing out here, sort of like people having camps or beach houses in Rhode Island."

He nodded. "Thought of that, too. I spent part of yesterday looking for titles or leases the Colliers might have had." He shook his head. "Nothing turned up."

"Do you think she could be with a friend?"

"I'm pretty sure I've spoken to all her friends, and nobody's come up with any new names to add to my list."

He leaned forward to bite into his second doughnut.

She felt her heart sink. "So where do we go from here? It sounds like you've done all you can."

He shook his head as he chewed and swallowed fast. "Don't give up yet. Talking through these cases usually helps turn up something new." He grinned self-consciously. "If I can't get someone else to listen, I talk to myself."

Feeling not the least encouraged, she tried to smile as she picked up an unused napkin from the small pile he had brought to the table. She needed a larger piece of paper than her small notebook to write on. Picking up her pen, she unfolded and smoothed out the napkin. "You talk, and I'll write," she answered his quizzical look while he finished his breakfast. "It might help you to talk, but it helps me to see things written down."

"Where do you want to start?" he said. "I've gone over this so many times in my own head, it might help if you ask me the questions that are on your mind."

"Okay." She thought for a second or two before saying the first thing that solidified in her head. "Why hasn't she phoned anyone?"

Ernie slowly sipped coffee that was probably cold by now before answering. "Assuming she's alive, and I haven't found evidence to prove otherwise," he added hastily, "I'm inclined to think you're right. I think she must be staying with someone, and either that person is lying to me about her whereabouts, or she's met someone that none of her other friends knows about."

Edna wrote the words STRANGER and FRIEND at the top of the unfolded napkin and added a question mark next to each. "It seems to me that she would still try to contact someone unless she's being held against her will."

He scratched the top of his head, frowning. "Not necessarily. Maybe she isn't thinking of the folks at home. She's recently lost her parents. She's probably still licking her wounds."

Edna shook her head. "I think anyone who has suffered a recent loss, as she has, would want her friends around. Loving faces and friendly hugs give you strength to heal." She thought again of Grant's first wife and how much being around family had helped Edna to handle her grief. Forcing the memory to the back of her mind, she returned to the current problem, "So, you think it's her choice to remain incommunicado and I think she's being held against her will."

She wrote BY CHOICE and BY FORCE on the napkin. She thought of Grant's confidence of the evening before. Was it Anita who had left the message on his phone the afternoon after her parents' funeral? Why wouldn't it have been? She decided to assume it was the woman herself who had made the call. She hadn't yet made up her mind, however, to fill Ernie in on what Grant had told her, not that it was much.

The detective's voice interrupted her thoughts. "Actually, I agree with you. I think she's being held against her will. I only threw that other idea out to see what sort of credence you'd give it. I'm inclined to think that someone must be preventing her from contacting her friends. I've thought so almost from the beginning."

"Do you think it's someone you've already spoken to?"

"Yep."

"Who do you think it is?" She felt her insides tingle with anticipation.

He frowned. "I think maybe Grant knows where she is."

Edna felt her temper rise, then forced it back down as she tried to look at the situation from Ernie's point of view. It certainly made sense, and the long hours he spent at the office ... Was Grant really working late all those evenings? Aloud, she said, "I don't think Grant could keep that kind of secret from me. I would have sensed by now if he weren't being truthful with me."

"Well, you asked, and that's my gut feeling. I don't have any sort of proof, mind you." Ernie spoke as if to appease her, then popped the last piece of doughnut into his mouth and wiped his hands on a crumpled up napkin. "What are your thoughts about Anita's disappearance? You've talked to some of the people she works with."

"I don't really know what to think. That's why I'm going through this exercise. I guess I'd like to talk to a few of the people you've already questioned. Maybe they'll tell me something they haven't told you. After all, I'm just a harmless old woman, mother to one of Anita's friends, not a detective." She smiled conspiratorially at Ernie.

"Who do you want to start with?"

"Her husband," Edna said almost without thinking and wrote Rice Ryan's name in large block letters on the napkin. "I overheard them saying at the office that he'll be at a restaurant in the Omni Hotel later this morning. Seems he spends a long lunch hour there every Friday. Arrives around eleven, if I remember correctly. I think if I drop in on him in a relaxed atmosphere and on his own turf, he might be quite talkative." She liked the sound of that, "on his own turf." It was something she'd heard on television.

Ernie looked at his watch. "I can show you how to get

there, but we have some time yet."

She nodded in agreement before she said. "What do you make of all the accidents that have happened recently? We know Anita's mother and father died in an accident. Lia Martin, a close friend, was killed in an accident." She hesitated before adding, "and Michele Davies, another close friend, suffered a fatal accident."

Ernie straightened up, looking uncomfortable. "Oh, gosh, I almost forgot. I heard from my buddy who talked to the kid that was on the slope when your daughter-in-law died. He says her death really was accidental."

"How do they know for certain?"

"Well, according to the official report, several witnesses said she was skiing too fast, hit a mogul and lost control."

"I know that's what they said. We got the report that she crashed into a tree, but couldn't someone have pushed her? Tripped her up somehow?"

"Apparently not." Ernie lowered his head and looked away from her. He was obviously uneasy with the conversation. "According to everyone they questioned, nobody else was near her. She was out of control, skiing dangerously."

Trying not to visualize the scene that had been replaying itself in her imagination off and on for the past ten months, Edna included Michele's name at the bottom of the list beneath a column labeled ACCIDENTS on her paper, but added a question mark to differentiate her daughter-in-law from the rest.

Looking at the names she had written above Michele's, she asked, "What do we know of the other accidents? Lia Martin died in a hit-and-run, but we don't know who the driver was, so we don't know if he did it on purpose or not. Have you seen a police report on the Colliers' car? Did it say whether the brakes had been tampered with?"

Ernie gave her a startled look. "What makes you ask that?"

"From what I read in the newspaper, I thought an inspection of the brakes might confirm whether it definitely was an accident."

He took his small pad from a jacket pocket and jotted a note. "I'm still waiting for a call-back from Nick, a guy I know on the force. He's the one who's been keeping me posted on the Martin case."

"Can he find out about the Colliers' brakes?"

"That's a closed case. It's already been ruled an accident." Ernie must have seen the stubbornness that she was feeling at that moment because he hurried on before she could speak. "But I also know a gal in the yard where they keep the wrecks. I'll ask her to look for me, too." He scribbled hastily in his notebook before glancing at his watch. "Since we have some time to kill, why don't I drive you over and show you where Anita lives."

"Yes, okay," Edna said. "Is it close to where Lia was struck down? I'd like to have a look at that park, as well."

Twelve

"Tell me a little about yourself," Edna said to Ernie as he drove out of the Safeway parking lot and turned west. She had learned that people in this part of the country tended to think in terms of compass points instead of left and right. Maybe it was because the Rocky Mountains provided such a gorgeous point of reference, due west. Whatever the reason, she was getting used to it.

"Not much to tell." His voice interrupted her rambling thoughts.

"You've mentioned a wife. Do you have children?" When he didn't reply immediately, she began to wonder why it was so hard to pull information out of him. Was Grant right? Did Ernie have his own agenda? Was there really a dying great-aunt back in New York, or was that a story invented to ferret out Anita? And for what purpose?

Again, his voice cut into her thoughts. "Two boys. Guess I should call them men. Younger one's twenty-eight."

She tried to picture the type of father the lumpy man in the driver's seat would be. "Do you have grandchildren?"

"Nope," he said after a second or two during which he seemed to concentrate unnecessarily on his driving. The traffic was light, and they were traveling on a four-lane-wide boulevard.

"Does your wife work outside the home?"

Again, his response was delayed. "Nope."

"Tell me if I'm being too nosy," she said, turning to look out the window.

"It's okay," he said. "Guess I'm more used to askin' questions than answerin' 'em."

"Tell me about your wife," Edna said, turning back to look at his profile. "I'm curious as to what sort of woman would put up with you." She grinned, then laughed aloud at the startled look he threw her. At last she had succeeded in shaking him up, if only slightly.

After another second or two, he sputtered a laugh. "Got me there." He paused and chuckled again before becoming serious. "She's been sick. Gotta have an operation soon. She don't say much, but I think she's scared. Guess I am too, a little."

At that moment, Edna felt her heart go out to this big, rumpled man, as she realized his feelings went much deeper than she'd given him credit for. For the flash of a second, he'd made her think of her own Albert, who, typically jovial and teasing, turned quiet and introspective when he was troubled.

"We're coming up on the spot where Lia was killed," he said, turning onto a two-lane road. The street took them through a residential area with an occasional car or truck parked on the street. Elm and cottonwood trees, towering over single-story houses, dropped occasional gold and orange leaves over the terrain.

She studied the passing landscape, waiting for him to point out the crime scene. When they had gone another mile in silence, she realized that he had purposely distracted her, probably because he didn't want her asking more questions about his family.

Finally, he slowed and pulled over to the curb. Ahead

of them on either side of the street was a greenbelt area bisected by a shallow stream which flowed through a duct beneath the street. She could see a graveled playground with brightly colored plastic slides and swings in the distance to her right. A paved path meandered several feet from the water's edge and curved upwards to join the sidewalk when the stream disappeared under the road. She stepped out of the car to get a better look at the site. Ernie came to stand beside her.

"There." He pointed to the left. "She came from over there." He moved his arm slowly, still pointing, as if following someone crossing the road. "She was hit about the time she reached the sidewalk. Here." His hand stopped and steadied on a spot not more than ten feet away near where the stream was funneled through a duct beneath the city street. "Impact sent her twenty feet into the grass." Abruptly, he dropped his hand.

Edna shuddered at the image he'd put into her head. It was such a peaceful place, quiet and lovely to look at. After a minute or two of silent brooding, she shook herself. "Grant told me it happened at dawn. Was the sun in the driver's eyes? Could it be that he didn't see her until it was too late?"

"From the direction the body went, the driver was coming toward us, more northwest. Not into the sun. He had to have crossed over to this lane to hit her. Struck her from behind, drove over the curb and back onto the street. No tire marks indicating he put on his brakes."

"Do I remember correctly that there was a witness?"

"Yep. Guy walking his dog over there by the swings. Said he was too far away to get a good look at the driver or the license plate, though. All he could say for sure was that the vehicle was a dark colored SUV."

"Nobody else around?" She looked right and left. Several houses and some apartment buildings were nearby. "Didn't anyone see the accident from one of these homes?"

"Nothing on the police report. Fella with the dog was the only one who came forward. He's the one dialed nine-one-one."

"Did he actually see the SUV driving toward Lia?" Edna was horrified at the thought of witnessing such a thing.

"Nope. Said his dog started barking and pulling at the leash. He turned just in time to see Lia hit the ground. The vehicle was on the sidewalk, heading back onto the road."

"What did he do? Did he at least yell at the driver to stop?"

"Said he shouted and ran toward the street, waving his arms. He'd let go of the dog's leash. Dog ran over to the body. When the guy realized the SUV wasn't stopping, he turned back to Lia and called in the emergency. Police station's less than a mile away, and the emergency guys got here pretty quick, but she was already dead."

Ernie leaned against the car, crossing his arms over his chest, and fell silent. Finally, Edna said, "I've seen enough. Let's go."

The image of the idyllic location for such a horrific death stayed with her as Ernie drove the few blocks to the complex where Lia and Anita both owned townhomes. Remembering how much the two young women had looked alike and what Grant had told her about Anita being the one to run at dawn, Edna said, "Do you think whoever killed Lia mistook her for Anita?"

He looked startled, as if the thought hadn't occurred to him. After frowning through the windshield briefly, he looked at her and shrugged. "Guess we won't know the answer to that until they find out who did it."

"Mightn't they find out who did it by looking for whoever had a motive?" she asked, thinking of the television crime shows she'd seen.

"I'll let the police work that one out. Right now, I'm more interested in finding Anita." He winked, taking some of the sting out of his words before he changed the subject completely. "I'm going to take you back to your car. The Colliers' house is on the way to Broomfield, closer to where you're going to meet Mr. Ryan. You can follow me from Safeway."

She had a momentary feeling of panic. She wasn't familiar with the area and had no idea of how to get back to Grant's from here or from the Omni Hotel. She voiced her anxiety to Ernie.

"Denver streets run pretty much north-south, east-west," he explained, then proceeded to give her a lesson in the numbered and alphabetically-named streets, with the odd-numbered addresses always being on the north and west. "At least in the older parts of town, before the dang-blasted developers started with their circles and horseshoes."

These last words almost undermined the confidence she was feeling about getting around the city. Good thing Grant had left a map in the car with his house's location circled and marked with a red "X." And she always had her cell phone, if she needed to call Karissa for directions home.

When they reached the Safeway parking lot, Ernie

wrote some basic directions on a slip of paper torn from his pocket notebook. First, they would swing by Standley Lake where the Colliers had lived. Then, he would drive to the Omni. On the reverse side of the paper, he added directions for getting back to Grant's house from the hotel. "Got me a new cell, too, if you need to reach me." He wrote his phone number in large numerals at the top of the paper before handing it to her.

She got into her car and at first concentrated on following him, making certain he didn't get more than a car length or two ahead of her. Eventually, she began to relax and study the street signs and, where she could see them, the numbers on the buildings. Glancing at the mountains to her left, resplendent in their peaks of white, she knew she was heading north and that the street she was on was Kipling. As she kept up with Ernie's white Ford Fairlane, she noticed the developments began to look newer, the trees younger and the houses larger, closer together. Most of the developments in the area had tall wooden fences shielding them from the street traffic.

"Oh, my." The words came involuntarily as her breath caught in her throat. Having followed a curve in the road, she was headed west and down a slight incline to a traffic light. Before her, the view opened up to reveal a large lake with snow-capped mountains rising majestically in the background. With the bright sun throwing sparkles on water that reflected the deep blue of the sky, she found the scene spectacular. She was constantly being surprised and delighted by the offerings of this western metropolis. Now, here was this gorgeous, big lake in the midst of sprawling housing developments.

Edna had time to enjoy the view for several seconds as

Ernie slowed down to turn onto 88th which ran beside the lake. Then almost immediately, he turned away from the water, making several more turns before pulling over to the side of the road. She parked the Toyota behind his Ford, and by the time she'd turned off the engine, he was opening the car door for her to get out. Leaning against the rear of the car, he nodded toward the house diagonally across the street. "That's the Colliers' place."

Standing beside him, she studied the two-story white building with its blue-gray trim. It was an expensive house in a quiet neighborhood. No cars were parked on the street, nor were any in sight. Nobody was walking a dog or puttering around a yard. It almost looked like nobody lived in the development.

"The Colliers had money," she remarked.

"Enough," he said. "Not nearly the fortune he was going to inherit from his aunt. Not enough for his daughter to retire on." He looked pointedly at Edna.

She thought for a moment, remembering her earlier suggestion that the Colliers' accident might have been planned. "I didn't say Anita tampered with the brakes of her parents' car," she said, feeling his accusatory stare.

"Never said you did, but I got the impression back at Safeway you might be thinking it," he replied, returning his gaze to the house.

"All I want to know is if the police found evidence of tampering." The frustration over too many questions and not enough answers began to build like a bubble in her stomach and edge its way into her chest. "Don't you think there's something strange going on?" She pushed his shoulder, throwing him momentarily off-balance. She wanted him to say something, agree with her, disagree.

She didn't care which as long as he started talking, telling her what he thought.

"Okay, okay," he said, regaining his footing and leaning once more against the old red Celica. "Yes, I think something smells, but I don't know what it is yet. Can't get my head around it."

"Well, how about beginning with all the supposed accidents that have recently happened to people close to Anita? Who would have a motive to kill her parents or her ex-roommate?" She decided not to mention Michele, since Ernie seemed convinced that her death was an accident. "You've spoken to all the neighbors?" she asked.

"Yep."

She looked at him expectantly, but he seemed to be concentrating on the house across the street. "I suppose you'd tell me if you've learned anything from anyone around here."

He turned to give her a curious look. "'Course I would. We're partners, aren't we?"

She was surprised at the words but found that they pleased her. "Yes, I guess you might say we're partners in this."

He looked at his watch. "We'd better get going if you want to be at the Omni by eleven."

Feeling the weight of her questions pressing down on her shoulders, she got back into her car, knowing she wouldn't get any answers from Ernie this morning. She kept his car in sight as they turned north toward Broomfield and the hotel that he had told her was at the east end of an industrial park known as Interlocken. His earlier description of Flatirons Crossing, one of the newer "mega" shopping malls in the area, did nothing to excite her. She was not in the mood for shopping, no matter how many or how grand the stores. Rather, scenes from this morning's tour whirled in her head. Images of the park where Lia had been killed mixed with the spectacular lake view, the Colliers' large house and Ernie's words, "We're partners." Partners. But overlaying everything was the one thought that always remained prominent: *Where was Anita?*

Thirteen

At the Omni, Ernie didn't stop when Edna turned into the parking lot but waved as he drove away. Proud of herself and relieved that she had reached her destination without having lost sight of his vehicle, she hurried into the hotel. She hoped she had arrived before Rice. It fit her plan better to be at a table before he walked in, nervous as she was over confronting him.

Off the main lobby, a pleasant young man greeted her at the wide entrance to the restaurant. At her request, he seated her at a small table where she could keep an eye on the door. She said she was meeting someone and would have a cup of tea while she waited. It was five minutes to eleven when she looked at her watch after the waiter left to fill her order.

Glancing around, she saw only three other people in the restaurant. A young woman dressed in a navy blue business suit was leafing through a stack of papers while eating a salad, and an older couple (retired, Edna thought) talked quietly over coffee. The waiter brought her tea and poured for her before setting the small pot on the table. She took a sip of the Earl Grey and was setting her cup back into its saucer when Rice walked through the door. He was studying the young woman, alone at her table, as he drew nearer to Edna. His selective vision would have ruled out the older people in the room. Edna was certain he hadn't seen her.

"Excuse me." She caught Rice's attention as he was about to walk by. "Don't I know you?"

He turned, frowning for a second or two before giving her a charming smile. "You look familiar to me too. By any chance, have you worked at Office Plus? Is that where I might have seen you?"

She forced a delighted laugh, hoping she sounded sincere. "No, but my son does. I was there yesterday, but I would have remembered if I'd met you." She waited to give him a chance to place her, feeling somehow it would please him to do so.

After studying her for a few seconds longer, Rice snapped his fingers. "Grant Davies. He's your son, isn't he?"

"Yes, that's right." She beamed as any proud mother would, she thought.

"We met on Wednesday, at the funeral."

She felt her smile fade, reminded that several people had died recently and that this was serious business she was conducting. Attempting another, less bright smile, she said, "Oh, yes. Mr. Ryan, isn't it? I remember now. Grant introduced us in the parking lot." She held out her hand for him to shake. "Won't you join me?" She was ready to hold onto his hand if he showed any intention of hurrying away, but he surprised her with his eagerness to sit.

"What are you having?" He eyed the teapot as the waiter approached the table. "This won't do. Have some wine with me."

Before she could decline, he was talking to the waiter. "Jason, bring us two glasses of your special Chardonnay and some nachos, will you? Oh, and put this lady's tea on my tab."

"Certainly, Mr. Ryan." The waiter went off, anxious to please.

"That's very nice of you," she stammered, feeling as if she was losing control of the situation.

He studied her across the table, obviously surprised to see her in the restaurant. "If you don't mind my asking, what are you doing at the Omni? Don't tell me Grant has you staying at a hotel." He smiled to let her know he was joking.

She laughed politely in return, determined to out-charm the man. "No, I'm waiting for a friend. We were supposed to meet for brunch, but I'm beginning to think I've been stood up." She didn't elaborate on her lie, believing the less said the better. Instead, she turned the topic to him, "And you?"

"Oh, I'm a regular for Friday lunch. I'm meeting some business clients. Boring stuff, really, or I'd ask you to join us."

The waiter chose that time to bring the wine and appetizer to the table. She preferred to stick with her tea but didn't refuse Rice's hospitality. He raised his glass in a silent toast before taking a large swallow.

She wet her lips with the Chardonnay and put her glass down. She knew his time with her would be limited, so she decided to get him talking about himself and move quickly on to his wife. "I've been fascinated by the mix of people I've met here. Grant tells me that almost everyone he knows is a transplant to Colorado. Did you move from elsewhere or were you born here?"

"I'm originally from Chicago."

She gave a tinkling laugh of delight. It was the sort of reaction she thought he might expect from an empty-headed older woman. "You see," she gushed delightedly, "my son is right. So, what brought you to Denver?" She picked up her wine and put it to her lips as he drank deeply from his glass.

"I came west to find my fortune." He gave a short laugh, apparently finding humor in his reply, before switching the subject to her. "Are you enjoying your visit to our fair city?"

"Yes, thank you." She wasn't letting him off that easily. "Do you have family in Colorado?"

"Only my wife. My brothers and sisters prefer to stay in Chicago." He frowned, looking into his glass as he mentioned his siblings.

She noticed the plural. "How many brothers and sisters do you have?"

"There are nine of us. I'm the oldest."

"Oh, my," she said, not certain what she had expected to hear, but definitely not so large a number. "That's a lot of mouths to feed." The comment slipped out when she thought of her own four children as teenagers with what seemed like bottomless pits of stomachs.

He snorted a curt laugh. "We weren't the wealthiest family on the block, that's for sure. Pop works hard. He's always worked hard, but he never seems to get anywhere."

"What sort of work does he do?"

"He owns a garage. I grew up working at the garage. My brothers still do. I'm the only one who left. As soon as my brother Joey was sixteen, that made four of us at the shop and Ralphie coming along in another year. I figured I could split and no one would miss me."

"Speaking from a mother's perspective, I can say that

probably isn't true." Edna's natural inclination was to reassure the man of his worth to his family, while at the same time she was thinking, *so he's been a mechanic,* and wondered if he might have fiddled with his father-in-law's car.

At her last remark, he lifted his eyes to her face and smiled. "Have you had a chance to meet many of Grant's friends since you've been here?"

She almost laughed aloud. Rice seemed to be pumping her for information as much as she was him. *All right,* she thought, *give a little to get a little.* "Not very many. I'm spending most of my time getting to know my new daughter-in-law."

He finished his wine and held the empty glass up, motioning to the waiter. She took the opportunity to broach the subject she was most interested in.

"I seem to remember your wife was a good friend of my late daughter-in-law. Michele spoke very highly of Anita."

He frowned, as if having difficulty pulling memories from the past. "Yes, I guess they spent a lot of time together, but that was before Anita and I were married."

Before she could reply, the waiter returned and set down a fresh glass of wine, taking the empty away. As soon as the young man was out of earshot, she slipped her question in before Rice could speak again.

"I'd like to meet your wife. Her kindness meant a great deal to my family. Would you know how I could reach her?"

A look of surprise swept the scowl off his face. "Hasn't Grant told you that Anita and I are separated?" Suspicion glinted in his eyes. "He probably knows where she is better than I do. The two of them have been chummy for years." He studied her face closely, as if trying to learn something from her reaction.

She felt her anger flare at his insinuation but tried to keep it from her voice. Remembering the old adage about catching more flies with honey, she said, "As a matter of fact, he did tell me about your wife filing for divorce, but he doesn't know where she is. Actually, he's worried that she hasn't contacted him. If you haven't been in touch with her directly, maybe you have an idea of where she might have gone or a friend she might be staying with."

He twirled his glass slowly between thumb and forefinger, watching the amber liquid. It was a few seconds before he looked at her. "What I think ... no, let me rephrase that. What I *hope* she's doing, wherever she is, is reconsidering her marriage vows. I'm sure she'll come to her senses and forget all that nonsense about a divorce. You see, Mrs. Davies, I love my wife very much. I want her back, but I think Grant is keeping her from me."

If you love her so much, why are you fooling around with Brea? The thought stuck in Edna's mind as she pressed her lips together to keep from voicing her opinion. Just then, the anger on Rice's face disappeared so quickly, she might have imagined his fury until she realized with a start that he was looking at someone behind her.

He waved and, as two men paused by their table, said, "Hi. Glad you could make it. Be with you in a minute." He waited until the men had been seated at a table near the large windows before turning back to her. The pleasure vanished from his face as quickly as it had appeared.

Fearing he was about to leave, she hurriedly repeated, "Is there anyone you can think of with whom Anita would stay?"

He drank the remainder of his wine in one easy gulp, wiped his mouth on a napkin and, bending forward over the table to rise, put his face close to hers. "If she isn't in Denver, then my guess is she's probably with her great-aunt in New York." He stood, a smile widening his mouth, but not reaching his eyes. "Tell you what, though, wherever she's gone, she'll be back next week for the sales meeting. I don't allow anyone to miss that."

Edna gazed at Rice's back as he walked away to join his associates. She had the distinct feeling he hadn't believed her when she told him Grant didn't know where Anita was. As she thought about Rice's supposition that Anita had gone to New York, her pulse began to beat faster, and she stared anew at the man leaning over the table to greet his lunch guests. *How does he know about Anita's great-aunt?* The thought struck her like a blow that left her breathless. Grant had been adamant about Anita's having no family except for her parents.

Edna grabbed up her tote bag and coat and hurried from the restaurant. In her car she fumbled for her cell phone. Snatching up the slip of paper Ernie had given her, she dialed his number. She listened with increasing impatience to the ringing on the line. Why didn't he answer? She wanted to ask if he'd ever mentioned Anita's great-aunt to Rice. After counting twenty rings, she angrily hit the disconnect button. Ernie had specifically asked her to call once she had spoken to Rice. He'd seemed eager, in fact, to learn what Rice might say. So, why wasn't he picking up?

Forgetting to check if a shiny black coupe was tailing her, she followed the directions Ernie had given her to get back home. She would have been pleased with herself for not getting lost on the way if it weren't for her annoyance at the detective and a new sensation, a vague feeling of unease. She couldn't identify its source, but a very real sense of disquiet was causing her stomach to roil.

Pondering her conversation with Rice, she entered the house and went down the hall to see what Karissa might want for lunch. Her daughter-in-law was on the phone when Edna walked into the bedroom. This time it wasn't the cell phone she held but the cordless that usually sat on the nightstand. Edna had learned early on that the cell was kept free for emergencies or for husband and wife to reach each other without delay.

"Oh, here she is now. I'll have her pick up the extension." Holding the phone away from her ear, Karissa said, "Starling's on the line. If you get on the extension in the kitchen, we can all talk."

The pleasure of chatting with her youngest child dissolved Edna's concerns of the morning as she hurried to the kitchen. She picked up the handset in time to hear Starling say to Karissa, "You mean he doesn't even come home for lunch anymore?"

And Karissa's reply, "He's been busy with the big software conversion project, and besides, your mother's here to look after me."

Taking that as her cue, Edna said, "Yes, here I am."

"Hey, hi, Mom."

The enthusiasm of her daughter's greeting warmed her heart while, at the same time, shot a pang of homesickness through her. "How are you, Starling?" She hoped she sounded as cheery as her child.

"Fine, Mom." She heard Starling giggle. "Actually, I'm

much better than Dad. He thinks you've been hanging out with another man."

Edna felt heat crawl up her neck and flush her cheeks. She was glad she wasn't where Karissa could see her. "Your father has an over-active imagination. He caught me at the grocery store. Probably heard some man talking nearby. That's all."

She wouldn't have minded Starling knowing about Ernie or about her search for Anita, but she didn't want Karissa knowing she was meeting with the detective. Word would certainly get back to Grant and she didn't feel like arguing with him again. She quickly changed the subject, asking how things were at home. After ten minutes or so of catching up on the news, Edna felt her stomach growl. Into a momentary silence, she said, "Did I understand you to say that Grant used to come home for lunch?"

"Yes." Both women chimed in unison, then laughed at themselves.

"He says he doesn't have time to drive home for lunch right now," Karissa said.

"I thought he ate at that little sandwich place he took me to," Edna replied.

"That was special. He wanted to take you to lunch, so he made the time."

"How long has this been going on?"

"A month or more. I guess since the project began," Karissa said.

Or since Anita's disappearance, Edna calculated. The thought popped unbidden into her head, at the same time she heard Starling say, "I should go. You two can talk about Grant's lunch habits without me."

"Oh, no," she insisted. "You and Karissa finish your visit. I'm getting off the phone now. I've neglected my duties, and Karissa must be weak with hunger. Love you, Sweetheart. Give my love to your father."

She hung up and set about making sandwiches and heating soup. Deciding to make extra to take to Grant, she filled a wide-mouth thermos with vegetable soup and wrapped up two ham sandwiches. She was setting their own soup bowls on the table when Karissa waddled in and eased herself onto a dining room chair.

The women ate in silence for the first few swallows. Soon Karissa put down her spoon and said, "Starling said I should ask you about raspberry tea for childbirth."

Her mind on the morning's activities, Edna had to think for a minute before remembering a conversation with Starling over something Edna had read. Hazel Rabichek, former owner of the Davies' house in Rhode Island and an amateur herbalist, had left her recipes and gardening journals for Edna. Since inheriting these fascinating books, she had begun learning more about natural aids for health and wellness.

She hesitated before answering her daughter-in-law. "I read an article about it recently. It seems that back in the Colonial days, women drank a tea made from raspberry leaves during the last weeks of pregnancy to speed delivery. They learned of it from the Native Americans. Then, during the Second World War, obstetricians found that an ingredient in the leaves, fragarine, actually helps to relax the uterine muscles."

"Raspberries," Karissa said and brightened. "Do you think I could try it?" Her eyes grew wide. "My mother used to tell me how long and painful her labors were with me and my brothers. She said I should expect the same thing, if I ever had children."

"I think you should discuss it with your doctor. Every woman is different, you know. You shouldn't worry about what your mother went through." She reached out and patted Karissa's arm. "I sympathize with you, Sweetie, but I'm very new at learning about herbs. Mrs. Rabichek put a lot of warnings in her journals. I remember one note on the raspberry that leaves not properly dried contain hydrocyanic acid, which is a poison." Seeing the horrified look on her daughter-in-law's face, she searched for something more encouraging. "There's something else in her journals about rubbing aloe on your skin to help reduce stretch marks. I'll buy a plant for you next time I'm out. They're easy to grow and, since they're also a succulent, will fit in nicely with the cactus gardens around the house. I keep one in my kitchen for treating burns."

Talk turned to house plants as the two women finished eating. After seeing Karissa safely back to bed, Edna drove to Grant's office to deliver the lunch she'd made for him, glad of an excuse to return to Office Plus. Maybe she would run into Marcie again. She might have remembered something about Anita since Edna had last seen the supervisor.

Entering the lobby, she saw Brea Tweed was at the reception desk again. "Hello. What a nice surprise," she said, approaching the counter.

"Hello." Brea seemed engrossed in a magazine and only glanced at Edna before returning to leaf through the pages.

Trying to remain cheerful in the face of the woman's rudeness, Edna said, "I've come to see my son. Is he available?"

"He's in a meeting. Can't be disturbed." Brea didn't bother to look up.

As she was about to put the bag with Grant's lunch on the counter, she heard someone come up behind her.

"Hey, Brea, where's the meeting?" A young man, stocky with thinning brown hair, approached and patted the counter a few times to draw Brea's attention.

"You're late, Wayne," Brea retorted, looking up with a scowl.

"I know, I know. So, just tell me where they're meeting."

Ignoring his impatience, Brea slid her eyes toward Edna, then back to the man. "This is Grant's mother."

The visitor brightened perceptibly and seemed to forget his rush. "Hi. I'm Wayne Freedman. I do contract work for Grant sometimes. Great guy." He held out a hand to Edna and she shook it.

"Freedman," she said. "Not an uncommon name, but are you, by any chance, related to Ernie Freedman?"

"My pop," he said, a conspiratorial grin spreading across his face. His eyes darted toward Brea and he said no more.

A bit startled that Ernie hadn't mentioned anything about his son working for Grant, she didn't have time to reply before Brea said, "You'd better get your butt downstairs, Wayne. They're in the IT conference room."

"Oh. Yeah." He dashed around the desk. "Nice meeting you," he called before disappearing behind the partition.

She stared after him, trying to figure out why Ernie hadn't mentioned his son to her. If Wayne's behavior had been any indication, Grant probably hadn't connected his worker with the detective he was so adamantly avoiding. Why not? She was pondering this strange turn of events when Brea's voice distracted her. "Wayne used to date Anita. Still has the hots for her, if you ask me."

Fourteen

After leaving Grant's lunch with Brea, Edna walked slowly toward her car, irritation and resentment building. Why hadn't Ernie mentioned anything about his son working for Grant or about Wayne's connection with Anita? Here he was, accusing her son of complicity in Anita's disappearance while his own son was probably having an affair with the woman. And another thing, was Ernie using Wayne to spy on Grant? *The nerve of that man,* she thought.

"Mrs. Davies!"

She turned at the sound of her name and saw Wayne hurrying toward her in the visitors' section of the parking lot.

"I thought you were going to a meeting," she said when he'd caught up with her.

"Yeah, I was supposed to, but Grant said they didn't need me after all." He shrugged. "He said he left me a voice message, but I was running late, so I didn't bother to check for calls before I left the house."

Despite her annoyance she couldn't help smiling to herself, imagining this son inheriting his father's organization skills or lack thereof, as it were. Thinking of Ernie fired up her anger. She decided to find out some things for herself.

"Does my son know who your father is?"

Wayne had the decency to look uncomfortable.

"Actually, no. Well, that is, I don't think so," he stammered. "He hasn't asked, and I haven't mentioned it. He's been pretty preoccupied with this big software project, or he probably would have made the connection, at least to ask about it."

She scowled. "Are you spying on Grant for your father?"

His eyes widened as he protested, "No way. I'm not jeopardizing a good-paying job. I told Pop that right off. No way I'm getting involved."

She considered his reaction for a lengthy pause while he steadily met her gaze. Finally, deciding on a different tack and watching his face carefully, she said, "I understand you're a friend of Anita Collier."

A small frown creased his pale forehead. Suspicion in his tone, he said, "Is that what my dad told you?"

"Actually, no. Brea told me you and Anita dated."

Wayne's cheeks flushed slightly. "I wish," he said emphatically.

It was her turn to frown. "What do you mean? You didn't take her out?"

"I wanted to. She was pretty friendly to me at work, like she wouldn't mind my calling her. I finally got up my nerve and phoned her one night. A guy answered, so I hung up."

"A guy?" Edna prodded. "Do you know who it was?"

"Yeah, I do." He sounded like a pouting teenager. "It was the guy used to go rock climbing with Lia Martin. His name's Yonny." Wayne snorted derisively. "Yonny Pride. What a ridiculous name."

The name was distinctive enough that Edna recognized it immediately and thought of the tall, dark-haired man to whom Grant had introduced her in the parking lot after Lia's funeral. She remembered the man's rugged good looks and couldn't help but compare him to the chubby young man in front of her. Besides a receding hairline, Wayne had inherited his father's portly girth. If he also had inherited his father's personality, women would feel comfortable around him, but she guessed he would elicit few sparks of excitement. A nice, loyal, temperate friend. She sighed. He wouldn't stand a chance of measuring up to a well-toned athlete like Yonny Pride.

"How long ago was this?" she asked, sensing by his reaction that the incident with the phone might have taken place fairly recently.

"Couple days before her parents' accident. I remember because I felt bad being mad at her after they died." Wayne's tone softened, and his face now showed sorrow and concern. Edna marveled at how transparent his feelings were.

"Have you seen her or spoken with her since then?"

"Yes, Ma'am, and I told Pop, too. I saw her at the funeral, at her parents' funeral, but I didn't talk to her. Lot of people were hanging around her. I figure she didn't even know I was there."

Yes, you would blend into the background, she thought. It was probably a good characteristic for a detective but not for a young man in love. "And since the funeral? Have you seen her since then?" She was getting frustrated with his vague answers. *Another inherited trait from his father*, she thought sourly.

"No, not since then."

She prodded him further. "Do you have any idea where she might be?"

He shook his head. "Pop asked me the same thing. Like I told him, if anyone knows where she is, it's probably Yonny." Jealousy hardened his tone.

"Aren't you worried that she hasn't been in contact with anyone for several weeks?"

"No." A hesitation. "Not really. Not until my dad said he couldn't find her. I didn't think much about it. She's away a lot, you know, on the job, driving around Wyoming and Montana and stuff. I wouldn't know who she talks to." He had returned to his pouting voice.

"But aren't you concerned at all that your father can't seem to locate her?"

"Nah. Dad's good at finding things. He'll get her."

After she had said good-bye to Wayne and he'd driven off, she attempted unsuccessfully to call Ernie before leaving the parking lot. On the way home she kept asking herself why he would have kept his son's interest in Anita a secret or, for that matter, the fact that Wayne worked for Grant. Just before reaching the house, she pulled over and parked, trying once more to reach the detective on his cell phone. As before, there was no answer. She double-checked the number he'd given her, making certain she hadn't misdialed. She wondered if he could have written it down wrong. Ernie had definitely asked her to call after she'd spoken to Rice. Puzzled and slightly disturbed, she drove on to the house.

Determined to put her worries aside, at least for a little while, she spent the afternoon pleasantly with Karissa and Jillian. When her granddaughter got home from school, Edna received another Frisbee lesson in the backyard. After she had managed to throw the disc straight to Jillian several times, the youngster cheered at her grandmother's improved skill. Only once during the afternoon did Edna manage to get away long enough to try reaching Ernie again, but without success.

At five o'clock Grant called to thank her for the lunch she had left and to say he was on his way home. He would stop to pick up Chinese food for dinner. Jillian helped her set places at the dinner table while Karissa talked to them from the living room couch. Everyone's mood was festive, and the party spirit continued when Grant arrived home loaded with small, white take-out boxes and extra fortune cookies. After dinner they played a game of Yahtzee and three hilarious rounds of Bonkers, Jillian's current favorite board game, before Edna finally declared herself exhausted and ready to call it a night.

Before going to bed, she reached for her cell phone and dialed Ernie's number, deciding that quarter past nine wasn't too late to try calling him once more. She almost dropped the small instrument when she heard him say "Hello."

"Why haven't you answered your phone?" she asked, keeping her voice low. She didn't want Grant to hear her, in case he asked whom she was calling. "I've been trying to reach you all day."

"The darned ringer was turned off." Ernie sounded annoyed. "I could have sworn it was on, but when I checked about an hour ago, the blasted gizmo had been switched to vibrate. When it's in the side pocket of my coat and my coat is hanging on a chair, I can't hear the vibrator. I tell ya, Edna, I'm not sure I like all this new-fangled technology."

Choosing to ignore his prattling, she cut in. "Why didn't you tell me your son works for Grant?" When the silence grew on the other end of the line, she went on. "And why didn't you tell me Wayne has a crush on Anita?" Crush might be more descriptive of a teenager, but it was the best word she could think of for Wayne's infatuation.

"How do you know about Wayne? Did Grant tell you Wayne was involved with Anita?" Ernie sounded as irritated as she felt.

"No. He doesn't know I spoke with Wayne and apparently hasn't made the connection between you two. I met your son at the office this afternoon when I took some lunch to Grant. It was Wayne who told me about Anita, and his feelings are pretty easy to read." She wouldn't let Ernie change the subject. "Why haven't you told me about him before?"

More silence before she finally heard him sigh. "Wayne has nothing to do with her. He has repeatedly refused to help me with the investigation, so there was nothing to say. He isn't relevant to our case."

"How do you know that?"

"Because I just told you, I've already talked to him about it. He said he hasn't seen her since her parents' funeral, and I believe him."

"Oh?" She felt her temper begin to rise. "So, you take your son's word for it, but you don't believe my son?"

"I know my son," he replied, but his voice sounded apologetic.

"And I know mine." She realized her voice had risen and stopped to take several deep breaths. When she felt calmer, she said, "Did Wayne tell you that he thinks this Yonny person might know where she is?"

"He mentioned the guy. I'm not sure how much

weight I put on Wayne's opinion. I know he tends to be less than rational when it comes to this woman, but I had planned to check it out. I've been trying to locate Yonny since Lia's funeral. Finally found out this afternoon where he's staying. I'm going up there tomorrow to see if I can catch him at home."

"Where does he live?"

"Eldorado Springs. The house he's living in belongs to a friend. That's why it's taken me so long to track him down."

"Where is Eldorado Springs?"

"South of Boulder. It's a small town up a dead-end canyon, about a half hour or forty-five minutes from here. It's at the entrance to Eldorado Canyon State Park where serious rock climbers hang out."

"Was Lia a rock climber?"

"Yes. That's how she and Yonny met. Apparently, he was teaching her some technical climbs."

Her interest was stirred. "I'd like to go with you when you talk to Yonny. Grant is working in the morning, and I'll ask a neighbor to look in on Karissa and Jillian," she said, thinking of Sudie. "I can probably get away by eight, and I think it'll be okay if we're back by one o'clock."

After making arrangements to meet in the Safeway parking lot early the next morning, Ernie told her that he had spent a good portion of the afternoon at the impound lot where he convinced his mechanic friend to look over the Colliers' car again. The initial police investigation had determined the brakes failed when acid from the battery ate through the lining. The cause of the hole in the battery was believed to be a small nut that had gotten wedged beneath the case. Constant rubbing of the two objects eventually wore a tiny opening in the battery casing. On more careful examination, however, Ernie's friend found that a hole had been drilled in the same spot—had purposely been drilled and the nut left beneath the casing, probably to distort the entry site.

She gasped at the news. "So someone actually did deliberately sabotage the car?" She realized too late that her voice had risen again.

"Are you okay, Mother?" Grant's voice came from the other side of the door.

"I'm fine, Grant."

"Are you talking to someone?"

"Yes, Dear. I'm on the phone."

"Say hi to Dad for me."

Not answering, she waited to hear Grant's bedroom door shut before speaking again. In a softer voice she said, "Have you told the police?" Even though she had insisted on Ernie's re-examining the car, she was stunned to hear that she might be right. The silence on the other end of the line lengthened. "Ernie?"

"I'm here."

"I asked if you'd talked to the police."

"I heard."

"Well?"

"Not yet."

"What do you mean not yet?" She was confused.

"Look, if they reopen this case as a possible homicide, I'm off it. The police will start looking for Anita, and I'll never get near her. What if they decide to hold her on suspicion of murder? Her great-aunt will die without seeing the only relative she's got left, and all that money will go to some veterinarian."

"But won't you get into trouble for not reporting what you've found?"

"I'm not hiding anything. My friend stayed after hours to help me out. Officially, she was off the clock and out of there. She said she could give me until Monday morning before she has to file a report."

"That means ..." Edna began.

"Yes," he cut in. "That means we've got only two more days to find Anita." At that moment, Edna heard a woman's voice in the background. Ernie said, "Look, Edna, I gotta go. I'll fill you in on the rest tomorrow."

She quickly reaffirmed the time they were to meet and disconnected the call, her mind trying to sort through all that he had just told her. She had slipped beneath the covers and was reaching to turn off the bedside lamp when her phone rang. Hurriedly picking it up before the jingle disturbed anyone else in the house, she spoke barely above a whisper. "What is it, Ernie?" She was certain he was calling back because he'd forgotten to tell her something that couldn't wait until morning.

"Edna?"

"Albert?"

"Who's Ernie?" Albert sounded put out. "Is that who you've been talking to for the past hour? I was trying to reach you and kept getting a busy signal."

She glanced at the clock. She couldn't have been on the line more than twenty-five minutes, but she let Albert rage. He had no patience with telephones and usually didn't even bother to call back when a line was engaged.

"How are you, Dear," she said, as soon as he paused for a breath. "It's good to hear your voice."

"Fine," he said. "I'm fine. Who's Ernie?"

She sighed, knowing she wasn't going to distract him this time.

"He's a detective I met recently."

"A detective?" Albert seemed to be shouting. She moved the phone away from her ear. "You mean a police officer?" But before she could answer, he went on, "Where were you that you met a detective?"

"No, he isn't a policeman, and I met him at a funeral," she replied.

There was a slight pause. "What funeral? Whose funeral?"

"A young woman who worked for Grant. He wanted me to go with him. I think he needed some family support, and Karissa certainly couldn't go." Remembering how Lia's father had bent to kiss his wife's cheek, she felt the lump in her throat she had experienced in the chapel. "Oh, Albert, it was so sad. All I could think of was that she was only a few years younger than Starling."

"What was a detective doing at the funeral? How did this girl die?" Typically, Albert ignored her sentimentality.

"She was killed in a hit-and-run, but Ernie is looking for someone else who works with Grant and who seems to have disappeared. He was questioning several people at the chapel, not just me." She thought Ernie probably had spoken to others attending the service.

After a brief pause, she heard her husband expel a long, slow breath and flinched, anticipating his next outburst.

Instead of shouting, though, Albert began to laugh. Soon, he regained his voice. "You do manage to pick up strange people in weird places, Edna. I'll say that for you. Why did he think you would know anything? Did you tell him you're only visiting and you'll be returning to Rhode Island soon?"

The wistfulness of his last remark made her realize how much she missed him. He might not be perfect, but she did love him.

He, in turn, sounded more relaxed, now that his humor had been restored. She didn't question his mood change. Feeling relieved, she proceeded briefly to tell him why a detective was looking for Anita Collier. She knew he would launch into a lecture about how she mustn't trust strangers, so she was careful not to mention her interest or involvement in the case.

Intending to distract him, she said, "You remember, Dear, Anita was the one who was so kind to Michele and Jillian when the family first came to Colorado."

He replied with some impatience, "No, I don't remember, but that doesn't matter. How's Karissa?"

Still thinking of Anita, she wished she could make Albert understand her concern about the missing young woman but thought she'd just make a muddle of explaining about the answering machine, the automatic paycheck deposit and bill payments as well as the ongoing customer orders. She knew her husband shied away from anything that smacked of modern technology or cyberspace. He wouldn't see things as she did, that a life could go on, but unless you made physical contact once in a while, how would anyone know you still existed, that you weren't just some virtual being.

"Karissa's fine." She felt deflated. She would like to be able to talk to her husband about her concerns but realized the futility of trying to do that when he was so far away.

She let the silence grow, caught up in her thoughts,

until Albert said, "Benjamin misses you. He's constantly under foot, and he's taken to sneaking up in the middle of the night to sleep on your side of the bed."

She laughed at an image of her cat waiting until he heard Albert's snores and then leaping quietly onto the bed. Normally, the cat wasn't allowed in the upstairs rooms. "I miss you both very much. It'll be nice to get home once the baby arrives."

She and Albert caught each other up on news from family and friends for the next several minutes before finally hanging up. Even though she was tired from her active day, she didn't fall asleep immediately. She was thinking about the tiny hole someone had drilled in the Colliers' car battery.

Fifteen

Early the next morning, Edna was awakened by the phone jingling next to her ear. Feeling groggy and only half awake, she mumbled, "Hello."

"Edna, it's Ernie. Sorry to wake you, but I only have a few minutes. I'm at the hospital."

His words wiped the rest of her sleepiness away and brought her upright. "Hospital? What happened? Are you all right?"

"It's not me. My wife's had a seizure. I've been here since two, and the doc just told me I can see her now. Called to say I won't be meeting you like we planned."

She looked at the digital clock on the bedside table. Six-forty-two, it read. Her mind began to whirl. If they don't see Yonny today, they might lose their last chance of finding Anita. The police would take over on Monday and wouldn't like tripping over amateurs in their search for a missing person or a possible murderer. She couldn't help but think that the authorities, once they learned of the hole drilled in the car's battery, would view the heiress as a prime suspect in her parents' deaths. She picked up the small pad and pencil she kept on the nightstand. "Give me directions. I'll find Yonny and talk to him." She hoped she sounded more confident than she felt.

"No, Edna. Thanks, but this is my responsibility. I'll get away later. Maybe I'll be able to get up there this afternoon."

She heard the reluctance and fatigue in his voice. "Nonsense. You should stay with your wife. She needs you."

It didn't take much more persuading for him to give her directions to the little dead-end canyon located south of Boulder off Route 93, which was also known as the Foothills Highway, he told her. He finished by saying, "I don't know the exact address, but it's somewhere along Artesian Drive, the street that runs along the north side of the creek. The town is small so just about anyone who lives there should be able to point you to the right house."

After disconnecting the call, she rose, showered and dressed, all the while going over in her mind what she would say to Yonny, if she found him. It would be best to get to Eldorado Springs as early as possible. She imagined that a young athlete wouldn't hang around home on a Saturday morning. Before leaving her room, she took a deep breath, trying not to think about how she would be deceiving her son in not telling him about her hurried trip to the mountains.

As it was, she didn't have to face Grant. When she walked into the dining room, Karissa and Jillian were talking in low tones over glasses of orange juice. Three empty cereal bowls lay on the table.

"Good morning, Edna."

"Mornin', Gramma."

The two greeted her in unison.

"I hope we didn't wake you," Karissa added.

"Now can I watch cartoons?" Jillian stood up from the table, one hand on a hip, looking sternly at Karissa.

"Yes, but please clear away the dishes first."

Jillian scooped up her cereal bowl and stacked it with

the other two before hurrying to the kitchen. As she dashed off toward the living room, Karissa called out, "Please keep the sound down." She smiled at Edna. "The baby got us up early this morning, but I didn't see any reason you should get up at the crack of dawn too."

"That was very thoughtful of you, but there's something I want to do this morning." She glanced toward the kitchen and the door to the garage. "Has Grant already left for work?"

"Yes, a few minutes ago. You just missed him."

Edna made herself some toast and poured a cup of coffee before returning to sit at the table. "How are you feeling this morning?"

"Fine. I feel really good, as a matter of fact. Once the baby settled down again, that is." Karissa rolled her eyes, but there was a twinkle in them, Edna noticed.

"I have an errand to run today. Do you suppose Sudie would come over to stay with you and Jillian?"

Karissa looked surprised, probably wondering what sort of errand Edna would have in a place she had rarely been before, but Karissa didn't question her. "Sudie is already planning on coming over later this morning for another sewing session. I'm sure we'll be fine. Jillybean will be glued to the television for the next couple of hours." She took a sip of orange juice watching Edna eat a piece of toast, then asked, "Will you be gone long? I think Grant wanted to take you and Jilly to the Denver Botanic Gardens this afternoon. It's supposed to be a nice day, and the paths through the gardens are very pretty."

"I hope to be back by noon," Edna replied vaguely. She suspected Karissa was full of curiosity but appreciated that she didn't ask any more questions.

Karissa hadn't exaggerated. The day was beautiful, warm and sunny even at eight-thirty, which was when Edna was finally able to get away. First, she had washed up the few breakfast dishes and made sure Karissa was comfortably situated on the couch. Jillian, sitting two feet from the wide-screen television and hunched over a large sofa pillow, seemed oblivious of her grandmother's departure.

When she turned west onto 120th, she was captivated by the majestic beauty of the Rocky Mountains before her. Off to her right, *north,* she mentally corrected herself, the sun picked out one particularly tall peak with snow lying in patches on the darkly rugged rock. Closer in, gold and gray aspen groves wove through acres of blue-green spruce trees, marching into the foothills and back along the Front Range. It was a breathtaking panorama and made the half-hour drive to Eldorado Canyon utterly enjoyable.

Turning north onto Route 93, she found Eldorado Springs Drive and followed it west until she reached the small town. Even at that hour, there were several cars heading into the canyon with her. Probably going either to the resort where, Ernie had told her, people went to buy jugs of artesian well water, or to Eldorado Canyon State Park where the technical climbers crept like spiders up the sides of sheer, five-hundred-foot cliffs.

She drove along the narrow road, keeping to her right as she had been instructed, until she finally reached a point where she would have to climb a rather steep narrow road or head back along the north side of the river that she'd been following on its southern bank. "Creek" was what they called rivers in this part of the country, she remembered as she turned downhill and maneuvered

Grant's little red Celica along the dirt road between cars parked head-to-taillights on both sides. She was thankful she was in a small vehicle and glad that there was no other traffic on the narrow lane. Considering the amount of activity at the mouth of the canyon, she was surprised to see nobody about in the neighborhood.

Houses clung to the side of the hill on her left and hugged the riverbank to her right. She drove slowly and carefully, hoping to spot someone and ask for more explicit directions. She had passed several houses without finding any place to pull off and park, when she spotted a man and a dog in the road ahead of her. Back turned, the man was tossing a yellow Frisbee to the German shepherd who leaped up to catch the disc in midair. The two frolicked before a small house which was painted bright blue and which stood not more than six feet off the road.

He must have heard the sound of her tires on the gravel, for at about that time the man turned, and she recognized him at once. Yonny Pride. She couldn't believe her luck. Slowing to a near crawl, she nosed the car into a narrow slot between the tiny house and a late-model Ford Bronco. As she did so, she saw Yonny shake his head and motion her down the road. When she stopped the car and turned off the motor, he approached the Celica, saying something she didn't immediately understand. She opened the door and stepped out.

"What did you say?"

"I said you can't park here. This is all private property. There's public parking where you first come into the canyon." He pointed down the road. About that time, the dog came running up, tail wagging and Frisbee clamped tightly in her jaws.

"Oh, I'm not a tourist. I've come to see you," she replied, firmly closing the car door and walking toward him.

Yonny stopped pointing and bent to take hold of the dog's collar. Frowning slightly, he studied her face. "Do I know you?"

She eyed the dog for a moment and decided she looked more gentle than menacing, so she turned her gaze back to Yonny. "We met at Lia Martin's funeral. I'm Grant Davies' mother, Edna." She extended a hand for him to shake.

"Of course," he said, after only a few seconds of studying her. Then, releasing the dog, he took her hand. "Sorry, I didn't recognize you at first."

She smiled. "No reason you should. I'm probably not someone you'd expect to see up here." She looked around, admiring the landscape. "It seems very peaceful for so many houses and cars clustered together. Also, I'm amazed to see so many tiny, well-tended gardens. It must be a labor of love in this rocky soil and limited daylight."

Yonny nodded, but the frown still wrinkled his brow. The dog nudged his hand with the Frisbee, distracting him briefly. He took the toy absently and replied, despite his obvious curiosity, "Most residents tend to stay home on weekends, but they enjoy being outdoors. Mostly that leaves them working in their yards. The canyon gets crowded on Saturdays and Sundays, especially when the weather's good." When the dog kept bumping his hand with her head, he said sternly, "Sit, Greta."

The canine promptly obeyed, and Yonny turned back to Edna, finally acknowledging her earlier announcement. "You came looking for me?"

"Yes, I did. I'm hoping you can help me locate

someone."

He turned his back and took a moment to hurl the Frisbee down the road. At his terse command, Greta ran to catch up with the missile. Only then did Yonny turn his attention back to Edna. A look of suspicion clouded his face. "You need my help to locate someone?" He repeated her words as a question, as if he hadn't heard correctly.

"Yes. I've been told that you're a friend of Anita Collier."

She thought she saw something flicker in his eyes but couldn't be certain, since at that moment he appeared to stumble as if his ankle had suddenly given out on him. She reached for his arm to steady him. "Are you all right?"

"Yes, I'm fine." He pulled free of her as Greta trotted up to them. "Recent injury still shoots a pain now and then."

She thought he sounded uncertain and wondered momentarily why he felt he needed to explain and why his excuse rang false to her ears. Mentally shrugging it off as her imagination gone haywire, she motioned toward his dog. "Please, let me." She took the Frisbee from Greta, thinking she would give Yonny a chance to regain his composure. Whatever made him stumble a moment ago didn't seem to her to be his ankle, but it did appear to upset him.

With her right hand, she leveled the disc behind her left elbow before flinging her arm outward, releasing the Frisbee at the last moment. It wobbled and fluttered onto the wooden walk in front of the house next door. Jillian would have moaned and hidden her face, Edna thought, grimacing.

"Good try," Yonny said, as Greta pranced up and

dropped the toy at his feet. After sending the dog far down the road after the flying disc, he turned to her, appearing to have recovered his previous mien. "Would you like to see some of the neighborhood?" She noted that his ankle seemed not to bother him at all when he started down the hill after his dog. They passed several houses in silence before Yonny spoke again. "Do you know anything of the history of this canyon?"

"Not a thing," she admitted. "Until this morning, I didn't even know it was here."

Yonny seemed pleased at the chance to play tour guide. "One of the more recent events that might interest you is that Ike and Mamie Eisenhower honeymooned here."

Delighted with this piece of knowledge about a former President she had admired, she said, "What brought them to Colorado? I know they met in Texas, which was his home State."

"Mamie's family had a winter home in San Antonio, but she grew up in Denver," Yonny said, obviously proud of the area and happy to relay his information. "Many celebrities have spent time in this canyon over the years. The Eldorado Springs resort was quite a hot spot in the early nineteen hundreds. Glen Miller played in the local dance hall." Yonny paused to look at her and added, "but that was before he became famous."

They walked on with Yonny describing more of the town's colorful past, pausing occasionally to throw the Frisbee to the tireless Greta. Edna was fascinated by the row of houses, built so closely together they seemed almost connected, and by the narrow canyon itself.

"Those walls are eight hundred feet high," Yonny

informed her as she stared at the sheer rock face opposite where they were standing. "There are some very famous climbs here. People come from all over the world just to scale these cliffs."

"Is that what brought you here?" She pulled her eyes from the view to look at him.

"Partly. I've read about this area ever since I got interested in technical climbing. When a friend of mine invited me to stay at his place, I jumped at the chance."

"So you're here on vacation?" She felt herself relax. The sun was warm on her face, and she was enjoying her visit with this personable young man.

"Sort of. I want to look at the veterinary school in Fort Collins before I leave."

Something in the back of her mind perked up when she heard the word "veterinary." She racked her brain until she realized it was Ernie's mentioning Anita's great-aunt's money would go to a veterinarian if an heir couldn't be found before the old woman died. That thought brought her back to the reason she had come to this canyon and with the thought came another: She must conduct her business and be home by lunchtime. She looked at her watch.

"I'm afraid I must be getting back, but before I go, can you tell me if you know how I might reach Anita." She had already decided during the drive to Eldorado Springs that she would give him the same reason she'd given Rice. "She was such a good friend of my daughter-in-law, Grant's first wife, that is, I do want to meet her and thank her for her kindness to my family."

Yonny rubbed a hand across the back of his neck before answering. "I'm afraid whoever told you I was

Anita's friend was mistaken. I knew her, of course, but only through Lia. I was giving Lia climbing instructions, and Anita came with her once or twice. I'm sorry, but I can't help you."

The disappointment must have shown on her face because Yonny put a hand lightly on her shoulder before she turned back toward the car. "If she happens to show up at any of the climbs, I'll ask her to call you."

Feeling as if the energy had left her body, Edna only nodded and trudged up the sloping road, back to her car. As she approached the small blue house, she noticed the sunlight sparkling off a stained-glass oval in the window. It was a lovely abstract design with unusual colors and fluid shapes. The window hanging seemed vaguely familiar, but try as she might, she couldn't remember where she had seen a similar one. Finally, with a shake of her head, she stopped trying, and her thoughts took a different turn. How was she going to tell Ernie that the search for Anita had come to a halt in this little dead-end canyon?

Sixteen

Perhaps it was the lack of information she was able to glean from her visit with Yonny that made Edna review every word and nuance of the conversation they'd had. Trying to hang onto the smallest scrap of hope, she realized that Yonny never actually said that he hadn't seen Anita or that he didn't know where she was, only that he hadn't known her well.

She had expected to be home by noon, but with the weather being so nice, traffic was heavy between Boulder and Denver, and it was nearly one o'clock before she pulled into the garage at Grant's house. Karissa was lying on the couch in the living room, flipping through one of her sewing magazines. She looked up as Edna came in from the dining room.

"Hi," she said, tossing the magazine onto the coffee table. She plumped the pillows at her back and sat up a little straighter. "You've just missed Grant. He's taken Jillian to the zoo. They left about fifteen minutes ago."

"How are you feeling?" Edna didn't think the young woman looked very comfortable. She felt guilty and didn't wish to talk about Grant, knowing she had disappointed him.

It seemed Karissa had other ideas. Ignoring Edna's inquiry after her health, she hesitated briefly before speaking in a low, gentle voice. "Will you sit down for a minute, please? I think we need to talk."

Edna felt the heat rise in her cheeks, certain that her daughter-in-law was about to scold her for staying away so long. Without removing her coat, she lowered herself onto the seat of an armchair, facing Karissa, and clutched her tote bag in her lap as if it could shield her against words.

"I feel that things are tense between you and Grant." Karissa raised a hand, palm out, as Edna opened her mouth to speak. "No, please, let me continue. Something has been gnawing at Grant since before you arrived. I think, in part, he's been taking out his anger or frustration or whatever it is on you. I thought if we talked about it, maybe we could figure out what's bothering him." Her eyes were pleading as she looked at Edna.

Hesitantly, and somewhat relieved that Karissa's intent wasn't to scold her, Edna said, "Have you asked Grant what's bothering him?"

Karissa sighed heavily, playing with some fringe on the edge of a sofa pillow. "I've tried. He says I shouldn't worry my pretty head, that I should think only about our baby. You know, stupid stuff. Anything to avoid upsetting me. What he doesn't seem to realize is that it's worse not knowing."

Giving herself time to think, Edna set her bag beside the chair, stood and took off her coat. Draping the garment over the chair back, she moved to the sofa, wrapping Karissa's feet more snugly in the afghan as she lifted them onto her lap and began to massage the toes beneath the yarn. All the while, she wondered how much to confide in her daughter-in-law. She was almost certain that Grant's moodiness was due in large part to Anita's disappearance. Eventually, she decided that Karissa had a right to know.

At least, she had a right to know what Edna had been doing and why. Who knew? Maybe Karissa would have some idea as to where Anita could have gone. So she began her story, telling her daughter-in-law everything that had happened, beginning with meeting Ernie at Lia's funeral service.

"So you see, Dear, why Ernie and I are so worried," she finally concluded. "There's no evidence or indication that anything drastic has happened to Anita, but nobody has actually seen or heard from her for several weeks. It would be a shame for her to lose her inheritance, but I'm no longer concerned as much about that as I am about just finding her, knowing she's alive and well. I'm very worried, and even though Grant won't admit it, I think he's troubled, too."

Karissa had been quiet throughout Edna's narrative, nodding once or twice, but saying nothing until Edna had finished. Now she said, "I knew Anita was having some sort of problem, but neither she nor Grant would tell me about it. I thought it might have to do with her marriage, but it might also have to do with her job or the company." She lowered her head, as if embarrassed. "I guess I really wanted to know if there was something going on between her and Grant. I finally got up enough nerve to ask Lia what she knew about it."

At the mention of the young woman whose funeral had been only a few days ago, Karissa's voice broke. She fumbled in the pocket of her robe and brought out a tissue. Shaking her head, she apologized to Edna between sobs. "I just can't believe she's gone."

Edna, startled at this new revelation that Karissa suspected Grant and Anita of having an affair, patted

Karissa's knee but didn't know what to say. She also had not realized that the dead woman and Karissa had been such good friends. She waited and allowed Karissa to gain her composure before asking, "What made you think there was something going on between Grant and Anita?"

Karissa gulped down another sob. Looking sheepish, she said, "It was probably my overwrought imagination, brought on by my condition." She looked down at her swollen belly. "I realized how foolish I was being after I heard Lia's explanation." Karissa wiped her eyes and blew her nose into the tissue.

"Which was?" Edna prompted her daughter-in-law.

"Lia was probably closer to Anita than anyone after Michele died. She told me that she had also noticed Anita's strange moodiness. It was when Lia and Anita drove up to Eldorado Springs to go rock climbing. That was on a Saturday, the day Lia met a new guy. I guess that happened about a week before I got up the courage to talk with her."

Wanting to verify what she already suspected, Edna said, "Was this new guy she met named Yonny Pride?"

Karissa gave a small laugh. "Yes, that was his name. She thought he was really hot."

Edna chuckled. "I expect he turns a head or two." Then, soberly, she led Karissa back to the subject. "Besides meeting Mister Wonderful, what else did Lia have to say?"

Karissa looked out the French doors at the back yard, seeming to be deep in thought. After nearly a minute, she began to tell Lia's story. "The three of them ended up climbing together most of that day, and then they all went to have a drink someplace. Yonny told them he had just arrived in town from New York and was taking care of a friend's house, another climber who has gone on an extended climbing trip to the Himalayas. Lia was pretty taken with Yonny right off, so she talked Anita into going back the next day to climb some more, hoping to run into him again. On the drive up that morning, she decided to find out what was bothering Anita, so she prodded until Anita finally confessed that she had asked Rice for a divorce."

Karissa turned to look at Edna with a small frown. "This is where it gets kind of weird." She paused before going on, as if to figure out how to tell the story. "Yonny wasn't around when they reached the climb site, so Lia and Anita started up the rock face. They hadn't gotten far when Anita's rope broke. She fell about twenty feet and was just lying there. As it turned out, she only had the wind knocked out of her and wasn't hurt badly, but Lia didn't know that at the time. Almost immediately, Yonny showed up. Lia didn't know where he'd come from. She thought maybe he'd heard her scream, but however it happened, suddenly there he was. He picked Anita up and drove them to the emergency room in his friend's Bronco."

Edna thought about how unwise it had been to move Anita, but that thought was pushed from her mind by another. *An SUV.* He wasn't driving an SUV Wednesday at the funeral, she remembered. He'd had to fold his tall frame into a compact car. Thoughts swirled in her mind, but she didn't want to interrupt Karissa's story.

"Anita was examined and had a few scratches patched up, but they were able to take her home that day. At the hospital, while they were waiting for her to be released, Yonny and Lia took a look at Anita's rope and discovered it had been cut. The end was only partially frayed at the break and it was pretty obvious that the other strands had been cleanly sliced."

Edna gasped. "Are they certain the rope belonged to Anita? Could she have borrowed it or picked up someone else's rope by mistake?" Edna herself wanted to make certain of what she'd just learned.

Karissa nodded. "Oh, yes. She bought her own rope when she started taking climbing lessons, just like Lia had. Climbers always take their ropes home and go over them carefully after each climb. They need to make sure the ropes haven't begun to wear or weaken in any way." She shuddered. "Their lives depend on those ropes."

Edna frowned. "So she would have checked her equipment after Saturday's climb?"

Karissa shrugged. "I guess nobody knows for sure, but she certainly should have. There's the chance she got distracted. Maybe she and Rice were arguing, and she didn't go over her rope, or at least not as carefully as she should have."

Edna got the impression by Karissa's tone that she didn't think it likely Anita would be so careless. Edna tended to agree as she urged Karissa back to the story. "Did they go to the police?"

Karissa shook her head. "No. Lia said Anita insisted they take her back to her house. Anita thought it was possible, even probable, that Rice cut her rope. She said he was angry and hurt when she told him she wanted a divorce. Lia and Yonny told Anita she was being stupid, that Rice could have caused her serious injury, but Anita insisted it would only make things worse for her if they brought the police in on it. Anita said she would handle it and refused to talk about it any more."

Karissa shifted on the couch, trying for a more comfortable position. Edna stood and helped rearrange the pillows before going to get her daughter-in-law a glass of water. When she returned, she noticed a faint trace of moisture on Karissa's upper lip.

"Do you want me to help you to bed?"

Karissa shook her head and sipped the water. "No, thanks. I'm fine. Just a little twinge." She smiled up at Edna, handing her the glass. "It's no easier lying in bed than out here."

Edna set the tumbler on the coffee table and went back to her end of the sofa, rubbing Karissa's feet after settling into the corner. She wanted to hear more about what happened the day of Anita's climbing incident. "Do you know if she ever confronted Rice about cutting the rope?"

"According to Lia, she didn't. By the time they dropped Anita at home, Rice wasn't there and didn't return for several days. We figured he may have been really angry or maybe scared, but also he might just have been away on business. Everything was so confusing about that time. Grant and Lia and I helped Anita move into a condo in Lia's complex a couple of days later, during the time Rice was away. I don't know if she ever mentioned it to Grant, but at that time I didn't know anything about Anita's fall. It was almost a week later before I finally got up the nerve to ask Lia if she thought Grant and Anita were having an affair."

"I don't think you have anything to worry about, my dear. I can tell that Grant loves you very much."

Karissa showed a weak smile and nodded. "I know. I'm ashamed of my suspicions now."

Quiet for a moment, Edna continued to stroke Karissa's

feet through the knitted blanket, knowing how good it felt when she had been pregnant and Albert had massaged her own feet. She thought about the story Karissa had just told her and tried to fit it into what she already knew about the people involved. She still had too many questions and not enough answers. "Did Rice know Anita was moving out? Could that be why he stayed away those few days?"

Karissa shook her head. "I don't know. I don't even know exactly how long he was gone or if he went to stay with friends or if he left town on business. I heard from Lia that a couple of days after we'd settled Anita into her new place, she told Lia she felt like someone was watching her. She said it wasn't anything she could put her finger on, just a vague feeling that was making her jittery. She was also getting calls after work and during the night on both her cell and home phones. There was no pattern to the times the calls would come or anything. The phone would ring, and when she picked it up, no one would be on the line. Anita had caller ID and apparently had also tried getting the calling number by dialing star-six-nine. The only thing that showed on the caller ID box was 'out of area,' and when she tried the six-nine bit, she got a recording that said the number couldn't be reached."

"It sounds like the caller had some sort of block on his line or was calling from a cell phone with a long distance number," Edna observed. "Did Anita ever report any of this to the phone company?"

Again, Karissa shook her head. "According to Lia, Anita said she wanted to see what she could find out for herself. Lia thought Anita was still covering for Rice. If it was Anita's husband who was harassing her, she didn't want to make matters worse by bringing any sort of official charges against him."

Edna wondered if it could have been someone other than Rice who was bothering Anita. "Did she mention her concerns to anyone besides Lia, do you know?"

Karissa frowned and shook her head. "No, I don't know, but Lia said the day after Anita told her about the phone calls was when her parents were in that accident. I talked to Lia the day after the Colliers' funeral and she hadn't seen or spoken to Anita since the service."

Edna thought about Lia's own funeral, which led her to think about Yonny. She then remembered Wayne Freedman's comment that Yonny had picked up the phone when Wayne had tried to call Anita. "Did Lia tell you any more about Yonny? Were they seeing each other pretty regularly?"

"They might have been," Karissa said, her brow creasing as she thought back. "We didn't talk much about her, only about Anita. She must have said something about him, though, because I remember Lia mentioned Yonny worked at a shelter for homeless animals. It's where he got his dog." She shrugged. "Sorry, but that's about all I know."

Edna thought of Yonny's comment about visiting the veterinary school in Fort Collins, when Karissa shifted nervously, drawing Edna's attention.

"I think there might be something else we need to discuss," she said, her cheeks darkening in a blush.

"Oh?" Edna inclined her head and raised her eyebrows. Her mind full of thoughts of Anita, she wondered what else Karissa would be so nervous about.

"I want you to know that I didn't steal Grant away from Michele."

Edna felt her eyes widen in surprise, and Karissa immediately lowered her own gaze. Her face was very red as she stammered, "I know you wouldn't ask about Grant and me, but I don't want you thinking I'm some sort of home wrecker. If you have questions, or if there's anything I can tell you ... " Her voice trailed off as she stared at her hands and picked at the polish on her fingernails.

Edna was quiet for a long moment, her mind whirling. There were so many things she wanted to know about her son's second marriage, but she never dreamed Karissa would open that particular door. The long silence must have disconcerted Karissa who raised her eyes slowly to meet Edna's, her cheeks still glowing.

"Well," Edna hesitated for a few heartbeats. "Since you brought it up, I had wondered why you married so soon after Michele's accident." Edna softened her voice, hoping Karissa wouldn't think her too accusatory.

"That was Grant's idea. Since we were planning to marry anyway, he said he saw no reason to wait. He said Jillian needed a mother."

That certainly sounds like Grant, Edna thought. He had never had the patience to wait for something, once he made up his mind to it. As she thought of his wish to provide a mother for Jillian, she thought back to when he had been young and she'd had to go to the hospital for an extended stay. Had he been affected by her absence? Were those past memories the reason he had rushed into this marriage?

As if reading her mind, Karissa said, "We'd been in love long before Michele's accident." Hurrying to explain, she added, "We used to eat lunch in the cafeteria around the same time. I ate lunch late because I used to fill in at the reception desk between noon and one o'clock. Grant preferred to eat lunch when the room was empty and quiet. Often, we were the only ones in the lunchroom. I liked him right off, but I knew he was married. We talked about a lot of different things and got to know each other pretty well."

"Did he talk about problems between Michele and him?" Edna hoped Grant hadn't been disloyal to his wife.

Karissa's eyes widened. "Oh, no. He never said a word about his marriage. It was just something I felt. Maybe it was something I wanted to feel, but I had a strong suspicion that he wasn't happy at home. He's such a wonderful man. I never thought he would feel the same about me as I do about him."

At that moment, Edna thought Karissa looked particularly beautiful. She understood how her son could have fallen in love with this woman. Mentally shaking herself out of Karissa's unwitting spell, Edna said, "When did you first talk about your attraction for each other?"

"It was at the company's New Year's Eve party last year. I only went because I got roped into working on the party committee. I don't really like big parties, and I didn't have anyone to go with. I didn't expect to see Grant there, but he told me later that Anita insisted he attend. She said the people in his department were getting awards, and he had to be there. She sympathized that Michele had been buried only three weeks before but said he need only stay until after the ceremonies. He ended up staying quite a bit longer than that." Karissa's self-conscious giggle ended with a sharp intake of breath, as she bent forward, clutching her bulging belly.

"Oh, dear. What's the matter?" Edna was on her feet in

an instant, leaning over her daughter-in-law. Her pulse raced with fear when Karissa didn't respond immediately.

"I'll be fine," the young woman finally stuttered, "but maybe I should get to bed."

Slowly and very gently, Edna helped Karissa to her feet and down the hall to the master bedroom. Edna's worries increased as she realized she was supporting most of her daughter-in-law's weight.

"Shall I call your doctor?" she asked, once Karissa was lying in bed and she had pulled the comforter up to her shoulders.

"No, I'll be fine. If you could just shut out the sun … "

Edna went immediately to pull the drapes against the afternoon sun that spilled into the room. With her hand on the pull cord, she stopped and drew an involuntary breath.

"What is it?" Karissa asked from the bed, moving as if to rise to the aid of her mother-in-law. "What's wrong?"

Edna nodded toward the stained-glass adornment hanging in the middle of the large window. The sun reflected through the swirling shapes and unusual colors. "Where did you get this? I saw almost an exact copy of it this morning."

"You must be mistaken. That was a wedding present from Anita. She makes them, and each is uniquely hers. You see, she draws her own designs and special-orders her glass because she's very particular about the colors. She's hoping to start her own business and get out of what she calls the sales racket."

"Has she given away many of these or sold them, do you know?"

"I do know. She wouldn't sell them. She's trying to build up her inventory. We're the only ones she's ever given one of her creations to. Not even Lia had one."

Edna didn't want to distress her daughter-in-law by disagreeing with her, but having an artist's eye herself, she was certain the glass art she had seen in the window of Yonny Pride's cabin had been made by Anita Collier.

Seventeen

He was lying to me all along, she thought, leaving Karissa to sleep and heading for her own room to call Ernie. If Yonny had one of Anita's glass pictures, and Edna was willing to bet it didn't belong to the absent owner of the cottage, then Yonny must know Anita a lot better than he had admitted.

If it were true that Anita had known him for such a short time, as Lia had related to Karissa, then why would she turn to Yonny for help if, in fact, that is what she has done? *Is she alive? Is she being held against her will? Why is her art hanging in his window?*

Edna thought back on her encounter of that morning. She hadn't felt particularly threatened by Yonny. She thought he seemed to be a caring sort of person. He was kind to his dog, and that certainly raised him in her estimation. His manner made her feel he might be slightly conceited, but he was not overly obvious or obnoxious about it. And he did have reason to be vain, she admitted to herself. He was a handsome young man, and women probably threw themselves at him. So why would he lie about knowing Anita?

What would be his connection to Anita? The thought kept spinning around in her head as she listened to the phone ring on the other end of the line. Why didn't Ernie pick up? Had he turned off his cell phone's ringer so as not to disturb his wife in the hospital? With that realization, she disconnected the call. She shouldn't disturb him. He had enough to worry about. She would go back to Eldorado Springs first thing in the morning and knock on Yonny's door. She'd find some excuse to get inside that house or straight out ask him about the stained glass.

She went back to the living room, her head buzzing with too many questions. Sitting on the couch, she tried to work things out in her mind, but she was so tired. Fixing a throw pillow behind her head, she settled back and closed her eyes.

"Gramma, Gramma, you missed all the fun."

Edna was startled awake by Jillian shaking her arm.

"Leave your grandmother alone, Jilly. Can't you see she was asleep?" Grant's voice, sounding as if he were suppressing anger, came from behind Edna. "Put your coat away and go clean up. Then check to see if Karissa needs anything, please."

With her usual bouncy step, Jillian skipped off down the hall, calling to Karissa as she went.

"Hello, Ma." Grant lowered himself into the overstuffed chair across the coffee table from her. "Glad to see you made it home. I thought you wanted to go to the botanical gardens with us this afternoon."

Still groggy from being awakened so abruptly, Edna was saved from replying to her son's implied criticism by Jillian shouting down the hall.

"Daddy, come quick."

His expression changed to alarm at the urgency in his daughter's tone. Pushing up from the chair, he ran down the hall. Edna followed, her heart skipping a beat.

"What is it?" he asked, rushing into the bedroom.

"I didn't mean to scare Jillybean," Karissa smiled

weakly, holding out a hand toward the girl. "It's really nothing to worry about. The baby's restless today, that's all. He or she just gave me a very big kick, and I'm afraid I yelped." She tried to speak lightly, but Edna could see beads of perspiration on her brow and upper lip.

Grant sat carefully on the side of the bed and took Karissa's hand. "Has this been going on all afternoon?" His glance hardened when he turned to look at his mother as if she were to blame for his wife's pain.

Karissa tugged at his hand, causing him to look back at her. "Your mother has been with me ever since you left. She has a right to some time away from here." When Grant started to protest, she stopped him by dropping his hand and putting her fingers gently against his lips. "No, listen to me. Edna's been here when it matters. She's been getting our meals and entertaining Jillian after school. This isn't a prison, Grant." She put her hand back into his and her look softened only slightly. "What's gotten into you? I've never seen you like this. It's unfair to think that your mother must sit at my bedside all day on the off chance that I might need her."

Edna watched the color begin to creep up her son's neck and into his cheeks as he lowered his head and played with his wife's fingertips. Jillian had moved to his side, and he slipped an arm around her waist, hoisting her onto his knee. "I think I owe all my women an apology," he said and turned to look at Edna. "I guess I haven't been easy to live with lately. I'm sorry."

Jillian put her arms around her father's neck and gave him a hug. "I still love you, Daddy."

The laughter in the room helped ease the tension, and Grant seemed to relax as he hugged his daughter back.

"I've had a lot on my mind recently, and apparently, I've been taking it out on all of you." He was still looking at Edna.

Karissa caught Edna's glance, but her words were directed at Grant. "Are you worried about Anita?"

Surprise widened his eyes as he turned to face his wife. He hesitated several seconds while he studied her. "Well, that's part of it." He looked again at his mother, then back to his wife before asking, "What do you know about Anita?"

Edna moved a small straight-backed chair nearer the bed and sat, saying as she did so, "I told her what I know about Anita's disappearance and what Ernie Freedman has been trying to do to find her."

He frowned, looking again from his mother to his wife. "Did she upset you?" he asked Karissa. "Is that what started the baby kicking so hard?"

"No, Grant," she said. "First of all, I told you, I'm fine. Secondly, I asked Edna to tell me what you wouldn't. I've been going crazy trying to guess what's been on your mind. I knew something was up with Anita, since she hasn't been around and hasn't called, but you won't talk to me."

"What's wrong with Anita?" Jillian's small voice cut into the conversation going on around her.

With a guilty start, the adults all looked at one another, then all eyes returned to the little girl's worried face. Since she was looking at her father, he was the one who spoke. "It's nothing, Sweetheart. Anita went off to be by herself for a while after her mother and father died in the car accident. We haven't heard from her, and we're kind of worried. That's all." He kissed the top of her head. "It'll be okay. I'm sure we'll hear from her soon." He stood her on her feet and rose from the bed. "Now, how about if we go get pizza for supper?"

"Yeah!" Jillian shouted and raced out of the room ahead of her father.

When Grant and Jillian returned from their errand, bringing home not just one but two varieties of pizza, the family all gathered around Karissa's bed and had a bedroom picnic, as Jillian called it. Edna felt better when she noticed that Karissa seemed to be resting more comfortably. She had been relieved when Grant agreed that Karissa should stay in bed rather than attempt the walk to the dining room.

Conversation remained light, and no more mention was made of Anita or of any other topic that might make Jillian think of Anita. Mainly to distract her granddaughter, Edna entertained them all with tales of her cat Benjamin and his new friend and neighbor Hank, a black Labrador retriever. After dinner, she played card games with Jillian, giving Grant a chance to spend some time alone with Karissa. Glad to call it an early night, she went to bed shortly after Jillian. Despite the nap she had taken, she fell asleep almost as soon as her head hit the pillow.

She was awakened by Grant turning on the overhead light in her room. Dizzy from sitting up abruptly, she fought to understand what he was saying to her.

"I'm taking Karissa to the hospital."

"What's wrong?"

"I'm not sure, but I think the baby might be coming. Jillian's still asleep, and I don't want to wake her. I'll call you when I know something." With that, he left the room and she could hear him helping Karissa out of the bedroom.

The sound of them moving down the hallway wiped the last vestiges of fuzziness from her head. Jumping out of bed and pulling on her robe, she raced to the living room, grabbed pillows and the afghan off the sofa and hurried out to the driveway. Grant helped Karissa into the back seat of the SUV and Edna made her comfortable with the pillows, wrapping the blanket around her as Grant got behind the wheel and started the engine.

In the house, after watching until the 4-Runner disappeared down the street, Edna was wide awake. The kitchen clock told her it was two twenty-seven, but she knew she wouldn't be able to go back to sleep. Worried and agitated, she brewed a cup of tea and sat at the dining room table, hoping it wouldn't be too long before she heard from Grant. She prayed that Karissa and the baby would both be fine. From what they had all said, Karissa was barely out of her eighth month, but maybe they had figured wrong. Then again, eight-month terms weren't unheard of.

Trying to stop herself from imagining the worst, Edna forced her mind to the window hanging she had seen at Yonny's, convinced that he knew more about Anita than he let on. She wouldn't disturb Ernie. His wife must not be doing well if he hadn't called to check in. With those thoughts reeling around in her head, she decided that regardless of whatever else was going on, she must return to Eldorado Springs as soon as possible. She had only this one last chance to find out what Yonny really knew about Anita's disappearance.

Eighteen

Edna managed to doze fitfully on the couch for a couple of hours and finally rose at quarter past seven to start a pot of strong coffee before heading for the shower. Feeling anxious about Karissa and restless to get back to the tiny mountain town, she had already decided that if she hadn't heard from her son by eight o'clock this morning, she would roust Jillian out of bed. After breakfast they'd both go to the hospital. Certainly someone would know something by then.

"It's a boy." Grant sounded both tired and elated when he phoned ten minutes before she had determined to waken Jillian.

"Everyone's okay?" She wouldn't let herself relax until she heard the words.

"Yes." He gave a short laugh. It was a wonderful sound. "Yes," he repeated, "Karissa and the baby are doing great. You should see him, Ma."

She laughed delightedly. "I plan to very soon." She chuckled again at her son's excitement, then asked, "How much does he weigh?"

"Seven pounds, three ounces. The doctor says he's perfectly formed and healthy."

"Oh, Grant, that's terrific news. How is Karissa feeling?"

"She's tired but looking forward to being mobile again. Says she can't wait to get out of the house to go shopping."

The thought of getting out of the house reminded Edna of her plans for the morning. "I was about to wake Jillian," she began, but before she could finish speaking the thought, her granddaughter wandered into the room, wiping sleep from her eyes with the knuckles of one small fist. "Who're you talking to, Gramma?"

She motioned her granddaughter over as she said to Grant, "Here's your daughter now. I'll let you tell her." She handed the phone to Jillian and watched the child's face light up with a wide grin as she heard the news. After listening briefly, Jillian waved the receiver in the air, tilted her head back and shouted, "I got a brother! Yippee!"

Laughing and rescuing the phone, Edna spoke to her son. "We'll be over as soon as we've had some breakfast." Before he could protest and just in case he had other plans, Edna put the receiver back into the cradle and instructed her granddaughter to get dressed. Mentally arranging her schedule, she decided that after seeing Karissa and the baby, she would leave Jillian with her father and head for Eldorado Springs. This was working out nicely, she thought, smiling to herself as she popped two ready-made waffles into the toaster.

At Lutheran Medical Center, she stopped at the reception desk to ask directions to Karissa Davies' room. She also wanted to find out if a Mrs. Freedman was a patient in the hospital but thought the receptionist might feel she was violating patient confidentiality to answer a question phrased in such a manner. Edna had learned a thing or two from Albert about how to approach hospital staff. Taking hold of Jillian's hand, she started toward the elevators before turning around to ask. "Oh, yes, and can you tell me which room Mrs. Freedman is in? The number has slipped my mind, and like a dummy, I didn't write it down." She looked sheepishly at the plump, elderly woman behind the desk.

If Ernie's wife was being treated here, Edna would try to find Ernie and tell him her plan.

"We have a Maxine Freedman in room three-oh-four. Is that who you mean?" The helpful woman stared inquiringly at Edna.

"That sounds right. Three-oh-four," Edna repeated. "Thank you." She had no idea if Ernie's wife's name was Maxine or not, but she'd find out. She smiled and began to whistle under her breath as she again headed for the elevators with Jillian in tow. She was really getting the hang of this detective business.

The next half hour passed quickly as she visited with Karissa and Grant. Jillian cooed over her little brother and thought he was the cutest baby she'd ever seen. "When can we bring him home?" she asked, looking at her father with barely suppressed excitement.

"We're waiting for the doctor," he said, studying his watch. He did look awfully tired, Edna thought. "She'll probably release Karissa this morning, and we can all go home."

That's my cue, Edna told herself. "I think I'll take a little walk around the hospital while you're waiting. I'd like to see how this facility compares to the South County and if I can take any ideas back to Mary," she said, mentioning both the hospital nearest to their new home in Rhode Island and her neighbor who worked as a volunteer there. It was as good an excuse as any to leave the room without Grant questioning her, but he only nodded absently when she picked up her tote bag. Before hurrying from the room, she added, "If I'm not back by the time you're ready to leave, just go along without me. I'll catch up with you later." She counted on the fact that he was too tired to process information quickly enough to question her intentions.

Out of sight of her family, she stopped near the elevators and tried Ernie's cell number. If he had turned on his phone's ringer again, she would double-check with him before walking in on a stranger, but there was no answer from his mobile.

Arriving at room 304, she rapped lightly and poked her head around the partially opened door. "Hello," she called. "Mrs. Freedman?"

A woman with short, iron gray hair was lying in bed, facing the window. As Edna ventured further into the room, the patient slowly turned her head and gazed blankly at her visitor. An oxygen tube was affixed to her nose and fluid dripped into her arm from a bottle hanging from a metal stand beside the bed. The woman's eyes were dark-rimmed and listless.

"Yes." The sound came from between dry lips in a quiet hiss. Then, squinting and displaying a little more energy, she said, "Do I know you?"

"We haven't met," Edna said, approaching the bed. "Are you Ernie's wife? Ernie, the detective?"

The woman on the bed gave a weak smile. "That would be me." She inhaled shakily before speaking again. "Why? Who are you?" She slid her hands down the bed on either side of her waist, as if she would push herself up.

Edna hurriedly put out a hand, palm toward Maxine. "Please don't disturb yourself. I'm sorry to intrude, but I'm a friend of your husband. I'm working on a case with him."

The slight stiffness went out of the woman's arms as she visibly relaxed. "Are you Edna?"

She found the question pleased her because it meant Ernie had told his wife about her and probably about the case, as well. "Yes, I'm Edna."

"Oh," Maxine sighed, the weak smile returning. "Glad to meetcha."

"I'm very sorry to bother you, but I've been trying to reach Ernie. I have news for him that I think he might want to hear, but he isn't answering his cell phone. Do you know how I can reach him?"

Looking toward the ceiling, Maxine moved her head slowly from side to side on the pillow. After a brief pause during which she seemed to be mustering her strength, she said, "I don't think he's gotten used to that new phone of his yet." She paused again before explaining further. "He went home to get some sleep. Been here with me all night. I don't want to bother him unless it's very important. He told me he'd be back about one this afternoon."

Edna followed Maxine's gaze to the clock on the wall opposite the bed. It wasn't quite ten o'clock. Trying not to show her disappointment, she smiled at the woman. "I'll call him later this afternoon. I'm so sorry to have bothered you."

In the same weak voice, Maxine said, "No bother. Want me to give him a message?"

Edna thought for a minute, before deciding. "If you could, please tell him that I think he was right, and I've gone back to Eldorado Springs."

"You've gone back to Eldorado Springs," Maxine muttered before turning her head away and closing her eyes.

Right, Edna thought, realizing Ernie probably wouldn't get the message. That was okay. She would call him this afternoon, when hopefully, she'd have something to report. With that thought, she quietly left the room. She hesitated for a moment, trying to decide if she should go back and speak to Grant again. The sooner I talk to Yonny, the sooner I can get back to the house and see that everyone's taken care of, she told herself and left the hospital.

On the way to the little dead-end canyon, she wondered how she was going to get into Yonny's house. She had to look around the place, had to see if she could spot anything else that might belong to Anita. When she reached Eldorado Springs, she drove slowly past the tiny, blue house, noticing no signs of activity. She stopped briefly to study the glass art which gleamed in the late-morning sun. She was right. Except for differences in color, the hanging looked very much like the one in Grant's bedroom window. She continued down the narrow dirt road, glancing back once in her rear-view mirror. Where was the Bronco Lia had told Karissa that Yonny had driven to the hospital?

At that moment she wished she was more knowledgeable about makes and models of automobiles and made a mental note to study up on them when she had the opportunity. If she was going to be any sort of detective, that was something she would probably need to know. Right now, she thought a vehicle of that sort had been parked near the house the previous morning. Maybe Yonny had driven off in it, or maybe it belonged to a neighbor. It was hard for her to decide with so many cars lined up along the roadside and so many houses clustered together.

Studying the vehicles along her route, she drove over the bridge at the end of the street and turned right. She hadn't spotted an obvious place to pull off and park on her first drive around the neighborhood. She would be less picky this next time. As she maneuvered the Celica down the narrow track for the second time, she thought that Yonny didn't seem like the violent type. *Besides,* she told herself, *if he had done away with Anita, would he still be hanging around? Wouldn't he have fled?* Interrupting her mental meanderings, she spotted a narrow space between a car and a tree. She was three houses away from Yonny's, so she pulled in and turned off the motor.

Sitting in the car and staring toward the house, she imagined herself knocking on the door to confront the man. He was young and strong and very fit. It wouldn't take much for him to overpower her and make her disappear, too, if that is what he had done with Anita.

Edna took a deep breath and reached to open the car door just as the door to the house opened and Yonny stepped out. Her heart raced. Should she confront him or wait for him to leave and try to get into his house? He was wearing a small backpack and had a coil of rope draped over one shoulder. Greta trotted out, and Yonny pulled the door closed. He looked up the hill in her direction and Edna, still uncertain as to what she should do, was about to sink slowly down in her seat when he turned abruptly. Whistling to the dog, he set off in the opposite direction.

She watched as the pair disappeared from sight. If she could get into the house and look around before he got back, maybe she would find something that would point to Anita's whereabouts. Maybe she could find out if Yonny was connected to the Quinn Foundation. The veterinary link was too coincidental, and she knew from her television shows that coincidences were suspicious. If, on the other hand, she found nothing to indicate Yonny was involved in any sort of subterfuge ... well, that would mean she was back to where she'd started, and she didn't want to contemplate that at the moment.

Now that she knew for certain Yonny was out of the house, she felt a surge of courage. She would just go see if he'd left the door unlocked. She would walk up to the front of the house as if she were arriving for a visit. Then, she'd knock and see if anyone answered before trying the latch. That's the way they did it on television.

Certain that the house would be empty, she got out of the car and walked purposefully up to the front door. If any of the neighbors happened to be watching her, she wanted to look as if she might be expected. She glanced in the window beside the front door but could see nothing except what looked like one end of a living room.

Pausing only briefly, she raised a fist and knocked firmly. She waited a minute, looking right, then left over her shoulder, nonchalantly trying to see if anyone was outside, coming along the road or standing in a nearby yard. She peered quickly into the window once more but could see nothing in the semi-dark interior. After several seconds, she took a deep breath, thinking *it's now or never* and put a hand on the doorknob. She felt it turn. Startled, she stifled a yelp as the door swung wide.

"Did you forget your key?" The young woman swallowed whatever she was going to say next and stared at Edna. Curiosity, then a look of puzzlement began to replace the smile that, a moment before, had brightened her face. "Do I know you?"

Edna thought it was probably the strong resemblance between her and her son that made Anita Collier feel they had met before.

Nineteen

Neither woman spoke for several seconds, Edna because she was startled to see the person she had almost given up hope of finding and Anita because she was apparently still trying to figure out if she knew her visitor.

"I'm Edna Davies." She finally broke the silence and added, "Grant's mother."

At the mention of a recognized name, the puzzlement on Anita's face morphed into pleasure, then just as quickly into caution. "I've told no one where I am. How did you find me? Did he send you?"

Assuming the "he" in question was Grant, Edna said, "No. Grant doesn't know where you are. As a matter of fact, he doesn't even know I've come here looking for you." At that moment, her surprise and delight at locating Anita switched to fear. A sudden sense of urgency made her reach out to the young woman in the doorway. "Quickly. We must leave. You're in great danger."

Anita backed away from Edna's impulsive gesture and started to close the door. "I know I'm in danger. That's why I'm staying here. Please go away."

Edna raised a hand, placing her palm against the door. "No, wait. Listen to me. You must come with me at once before Yonny returns."

Anger brought a flush to Anita's cheeks. "I don't know what you're talking about. Yonny's my friend. He's helping me."

That admission confused Edna. "Helping you?" She shook her head in bewilderment. "How is he helping you?"

Anita's eyes narrowed. Instead of answering the question, she threw one back. "Why are you here?"

"I came to find you or to find out what has happened to you. I must admit, though, I never expected to see you here." Edna knew she wasn't making much sense. She started again. "Look, I know about your parents' car crash and about the person who's been harassing you. I think Yonny is the one who's behind it."

Anita's face splotched with anger. "Now you look. Yonny told me the crash that killed my folks wasn't an accident. Why would he have said that if he did it? Why would he be looking for my stalker? And why would he have brought me up here and kept me safe?" Her voice had risen with each question.

How does Yonny know the Colliers didn't die by accident? Edna wondered at the same time she said aloud, "Did he tell you why someone might want to harm you or your parents?"

"He said I have a great-aunt back in New York who is going to leave me all her money. He says I need to stay here, where it's safe, until he finds whoever is after me."

Edna paused, her confusion increasing. *Could I be wrong about Yonny? But how does he know the Colliers' car was tampered with? Not even the mechanic at the impound lot knew until recently. And how does Yonny know about Mrs. Maitland and the inheritance?*

"Tell Grant I'll call him as soon as I can. Now, please, you really must go." Anita stepped back to shut the door.

Edna felt anxiety turning to acid in her stomach. She

was convinced this woman was in danger. "Please trust me," she begged, sliding one foot beside the doorjamb and pushing against the door with her hand. "If you'll only come with me to Grant's house, I'll explain on the way, but we must leave immediately."

"I told you, I'm safe here. Please move your foot." Anita lowered her gaze and prodded Edna's shoe with the toe of a sturdy hiking boot.

In desperation, Edna blurted out, "Do you know your great-aunt is dying?"

Anita stopped nudging and raised her eyes, studying Edna's face before her frown deepened. "You're wrong. I'm going to meet her as soon as Yonny finds out who murdered my parents. He says it isn't safe for me to leave here until then."

"So he told you about your great-aunt and your inheritance," Edna spoke the thought more to herself than to Anita. *If he has an ulterior motive, why would Yonny tell her all this?*

Anita used her boot to push Edna's foot away from the doorjamb and shut the door just as another idea occurred to Edna. "Did he tell you if you don't see your great-aunt before she dies that the money will go to the Quinn Foundation?" She shouted the name at the closed door.

As the echo of her words faded into the ensuing silence, she stood looking at the house for several more seconds, feeling desperate and helpless. She had done her best. Maybe Ernie could come up and convince Anita to leave this place. She was about to turn away when she heard the latch click and the door creaked slowly open.

"The Quinn Foundation?" Anita repeated the name, standing once more in the doorway.

Her glance moved to a point beyond Edna's left shoulder and her eyes grew wide. At the same moment, Edna felt something cold and wet nuzzle into her hand. She looked down to see Greta staring up at her. Giving a startled cry, she spun around to find Yonny Pride striding up behind her.

"How about we go into the house and stop entertaining the neighbors?" Yonny said, pushing Edna roughly through the door ahead of him.

Stepping back to let them pass, Anita stared at Yonny. "You work for the Quinn Foundation," she said in a tone that sounded both puzzled and accusatory.

He moved into the dark, wood-paneled living room, still urging Edna forward. Greta, who had trotted into the house ahead of the small group, turned and began to bark at her master.

"Quiet, Greta," Yonny commanded. "Sit."

The German shepherd backed away, continuing to bark. Edna thought the dog might be agitated by the hostility in the air.

"Anita, put Greta in the backyard," Yonny said, laying a restraining hand on Edna's shoulder.

After a momentary pause during which her eyes never left his face, Anita finally lowered her gaze and strode through an open doorway into a small kitchen at the back of the house, calling for the dog to follow. She picked something out of a tin canister on the shelf and bent to give it to Greta before opening the back door. The dog bounded outside with her prize.

When Anita returned to the living room, her questioning eyes again sought Yonny's face. Edna shrugged out of Yonny's grasp and moved away from him, rubbing the spot where his steel grip had bruised her shoulder. Anita and Yonny, both tall and slender, seemed to tower over her in the small room. The only light came from the east-facing window that held Anita's stained glass creation and from the north-facing window next to the front door. Seeing that Anita had left the door slightly ajar, Edna was wondering if she could slip by Yonny and scoot out to the road when Anita's voice broke the silence.

"Is it true? Will the Quinn Foundation inherit my great-aunt's money if I don't?"

Edna looked from one face to the other. Anita was clearly now more puzzled than angry. Yonny's face was set in a scowl. He ignored Anita's question and turned to Edna. "Why did you have to meddle? Everything was going just fine until you came along."

"Why did you have to kill Anita's parents?" Edna stared back, hoping he couldn't see the fear that was causing her heart to thud against her chest.

Yonny's head jerked back as if he'd been slapped in the face. "Kill the Colliers? What are you talking about?"

"You told her their crash wasn't an accident. How did you know if you weren't the one who caused it?"

Yonny looked at Edna as if she had lost her mind. "That was something I made up. Are you telling me it really wasn't an accident?"

"Oh, come now. Do you expect the police will believe your confession to Anita was only a story you concocted?" She felt annoyed at the naïve act this arrogant young man was pulling.

He shook his head in disbelief. "I used the crash to convince her that her life was in danger so she'd come with me. I didn't want to have to use force."

"What?" Anita hit Yonny's shoulder with the palm of her hand, making him turn toward her. "What are you saying, that my parents weren't killed? You lied to get me up here?"

Edna put a hand on Anita's arm. "They were killed. It wasn't an accident." But neither of the others was listening to her.

Yonny rubbed the back of his neck with one hand, apparently not wanting to look Anita in the eye. When he did, his face was set in resolve. "Yes. Okay? Yes, I lied to get you up here and kept lying to keep you here. At least it was easier on both of us than tying you up and having to watch you every minute of the day. I don't think I could have done that."

Anita turned to Edna with an exasperated sigh. "Let's go. I'll get my things, and you can fill me in on our way back to Denver."

Yonny grabbed Anita's wrist before she could move. "You're not going anywhere. You're both staying right here until I get a phone call from Dr. Quinn."

"A call telling you that Mrs. Maitland is dead." Edna voiced the thought his words had put into her head.

"That's right. I'm to keep Anita here until then, until Dr. Quinn tells me it's okay to let her go. Now, if you ladies will just have a seat, I'm sure we'll only have to be here a day or two more at the most." He gestured to two low-backed stuffed chairs on either side of the large window, but neither woman moved.

"Look, Yonny." Edna was trying to think fast. What could she say that might make him see reason? "So far, you haven't held anyone against her will, but if you continue with this absurd notion of yours, you'll be kidnapping us. That's a very serious crime."

Yonny looked frustrated but determined. "I don't want to hurt either of you, but I will do whatever I have to. You cannot leave this house until I hear from Dr. Quinn."

"Why don't you call him?" Edna suggested. "If he's your employer, I'm certain he wouldn't approve of what you're doing."

Yonny gave a short laugh. "Are you kidding? My instructions from him were to see that none of the Colliers got to New York before Mrs. Maitland dies. I don't think he figured I could do that without using some strong-arm tactics, do you?"

Anita had been quiet during this conversation, but now she cut in. "So you haven't even been looking for the person who was stalking me? Everything's been one big fat lie, and I could have gone to Lia's funeral?" Her voice broke on those last words as if she were about to cry, but she sucked her breath in sharply, refusing to give way to her emotions.

The corner of Yonny's lip went up in a sneer. "It's pretty easy to guess who's after you. That jerk you married is none too subtle when it comes to money or women."

"If that's true, if you think Rice is responsible for the Colliers' deaths, then let's go to the police." Edna's attempt to make Yonny see reason got no further.

"Nobody's going anywhere," came a voice from the front door as Rice Ryan pushed through the entry.

Since most of the light was behind Rice, it took Edna several seconds to realize he held a gun in his hand. Involuntarily, she clutched her tote bag tightly against her chest and moved closer to Anita. The small room had just become very crowded.

Twenty

"Good idea you have, keeping everyone here." Rice waggled the gun at Yonny. "Now move over there." With his free hand he pushed the other man forward, causing Yonny to stumble into Anita. As he wrapped his arms around Rice's wife to steady them both, Edna could see anger spark in Rice's eyes.

"So here's where you've been setting up house," he snarled at Anita.

"How did you find me?" she asked, ignoring his remark.

He tipped his head toward Edna. "I've been following her."

Edna gasped. "You're the one in the black car, the one I kept seeing everywhere I went." She frowned. "At the funeral you were driving a silver car."

He snorted. "That was Marcie's Lexus. I drove, but it was her car." He looked over at his wife, still in the protective circle of Yonny's arm. Sneering, he turned back to Edna and said, "I figured Grant knew where my wife was hiding, and sooner or later one of you would lead me to her. Since he's been spending most of his time at the office, I decided to follow you. Paid off, too, didn't it?" His smirk turned to a frown as glared at Anita. "Might have known you'd taken up with someone."

"You're a fine one to talk." Anita's voice was low and quiet but filled with loathing.

"I realized my mistake. I told you I would have done anything to get you back, but you wouldn't listen." Fury flared in his words, but his tone also held a hint of pleading.

"I got tired of listening to your lies, Rice." Anita sounded weary.

Edna knew from their looks and tones that Anita and her husband had had this argument before, probably many times. She thought she might take Rice unaware, reason with him while he was distracted by his wife. She took a step toward the door, eyeing the gun. "I know you for a sensible man," she said, inching forward slowly. "I know you don't want to kidnap us."

She was almost beside him, ready to break into a quick stride to reach the open front door, when he grabbed her shoulder and flung her roughly toward the chair beside the east window. "Sit over there and shut up," he growled, his eyes still on his wife. "You're not going anywhere. Nobody's leaving here."

She stumbled to the window but didn't sit. Steadying herself, she was about to speak when Anita's voice rang out in the small room.

"Did you kill my parents?"

"That was an accident," Rice retorted.

Edna scoffed. "That was no accident. The battery was rigged to drip acid on the brake linings."

Rice glowered at her, and in the light from the window behind her, she saw hatred mottle his face before he turned back to Anita. "Yes, I drilled a hole in the battery, but it wasn't meant to kill them. I wanted the car to crash and at the worst have one or both of them end up in the hospital. I didn't mean for them to die." He looked as if he genuinely wanted Anita to believe him.

"Why?" Anita's eyes swam with unshed tears, and the single word she uttered hung in the silent room. Everyone stood still, waiting to hear what Rice had to say.

Finally, he rubbed the back of his neck with his left hand while his right, slackening its grip slightly on the gun, dropped to his side. "I didn't mean for them to die," he repeated before looking at Anita again. "I thought if one of them got hurt, you'd need me, take me back. I would have handled everything. Doctors, hospital bills, everything. You would have wanted me to comfort you. We'd have been back together, and I could show you what a good husband I can be."

Anita swiped at her tears with fingertips as she shouted at Rice. "You bastard! You killed my parents. I'll never come back to you."

Edna saw the anger almost visibly rise up Rice's neck to his face. Her stomach lurched when she saw him raise the gun and point it at his wife. Apparently, Yonny felt the same as she, that they must somehow divert Rice's attention. The young man stepped forward, gently pushing Anita so she was partially hidden behind him.

"Were you the one who cut her climbing rope?" His tone was quiet, but there was a hard edge to his question.

Rice's eyes fixed on Yonny's face for several seconds as if he were trying to make sense of the words. Then he gave a short laugh. "That was nothing. I cut it through enough so it would break under her weight. She wouldn't have gone five feet up before it broke." His gaze shifted to Anita. "I did it for us, Baby. I thought if you stopped spending so much time climbing those stupid rocks that there would be time for us to do stuff together. Now do you see how much I wanted you back?"

Anita pushed Yonny out of her way. Bending slightly at her waist with hands on her hips, she leaned toward her husband. "You wanted me back enough to kill me? What sort of man are you? Do you seriously think after all this that I would ever want you back?"

Watching Rice's knuckles turn white and his finger twitch on the trigger of the gun, Edna spoke quietly to Anita. "You might want to reconsider."

"I'd rather die than live with you and your women and your lies and … and your psychotic behavior," she shouted at him. She seemed to run out of steam then and turned her face into Yonny's chest.

When Yonny put his arm around Anita's shoulders in a reflexive motion, Edna thought Rice was going to shoot them right there on the spot. She gasped an involuntary "No."

He glanced over at her, paused, then nodded. "You're right. Not now. I have to think of how I want this to play out." He looked the three over with a smile of satisfaction slowly spreading across his face. "Definite murder-suicide here," he said. His gaze fell on Edna, making her shudder. "And oh, how unfortunate that Grant Davies' mother should walk in on it." He feigned a look of sorrow before his eyes hardened and he gave a bark of laughter. "That'll take care of the kidnapping charge." He winked at her. At that moment Edna thought it possible that she could shoot another human being, if only the gun were in her hands.

Rice returned his attention to Anita, who had raised her head from Yonny's shoulder and was staring at her husband with a look of pure disgust. "You couldn't. Obviously, you can rig accidents, but I don't believe you could pull a trigger while someone is looking you in the eye." She shrugged Yonny's arm off from around her shoulders and stood before Rice in a posture of defiance.

"Considering what I have to gain, I think I'm capable of just about anything," he jeered back at her.

"What is that supposed to mean?" Anita's bravado wilted a little. "What do you have to gain except your freedom? You had that anyway, despite your marriage vows."

"I think he's talking about your inheritance," Edna cut in quietly. She had been watching Rice's gun hand and studying his face.

Anita turned a puzzled look on Edna. "How would he know about that? I wasn't even aware of it until Yonny told me."

Rice laughed with what seemed like real amusement. "You are so naïve, Sweetie. Don't you know I wouldn't have married anyone without having her fully investigated?" At her look of amazement he laughed again. "The first time I met your father—remember, he came to visit you in the office when you were still my secretary? I knew right off that he came from money. The way he dressed, the way he walked and talked. Written all over him. It made me curious as to where and how he grew up."

"You investigated my family?" Anita's eyes grew wide with disbelief.

"Of course, Sweetheart. I just told you that I wouldn't have married you if I'd thought you were poor." He shrugged. "I was going to ask you out. I just wouldn't have proposed unless there was a good reason."

"So that's why you turned on the charm so suddenly."

"Naturally. I couldn't let anyone else walk off with my millions, now could I?" He laughed again, obviously enjoying the joke on his wife.

Thinking it might prove a way out of their dilemma, Edna said. "You can't inherit. Only Anita can. If you kill her, there go your millions, as you choose to phrase it."

"What are you talking about?" Rice turned to her, the look of triumph still on his face. "You know nothing about it."

"She's right," Yonny broke in. "Mrs. Maitland's will stipulates that her nephew must show up before she dies. If he's no longer alive or capable of making the trip, then one of his children must come to her. If nobody appears, the entire fortune goes to The Quinn Foundation."

Rice spun on him, pointing the gun at Yonny's forehead. "Just who the hell are you? You know nothing about this, so keep your mouth shut." He was beginning to lose his temper again.

"He's right," Edna said, trying to take Rice's attention from Yonny. "Whoever shows up must be a blood relative."

Rice turned to her, looking thoughtful for several seconds. "Easy enough," he finally said, his smirk returning. "I'll tell her Anita has been unavoidably detained, that I'm her husband and we want to take care of her. As long as your bodies aren't found before the old witch dies ... well, maybe I can hurry that along, too."

"You won't get past her front gate," Yonny snarled.

"I told you to shut up," Taking a step forward, Rice extended his arm, holding the gun mere inches from Yonny's forehead.

"So you only married me for my money. You lied even

when you said you loved me."

As Anita drew Rice's attention from Yonny, Edna realized she had been holding her breath. She let it out slowly, watching husband and wife face off once more.

Rice had backed several steps away from Yonny before turning on his wife, destroying the hope Edna had that the younger man might grab the gun and somehow disarm Rice. She was drawn back to the argument.

"At first, yes, it was a lie, but I fell in love with you. I didn't realize how much until you left me." His face looked truly sad for a split second, Edna thought without feeling the least bit sorry for him.

Anita's eyes narrowed as she snarled at her husband, "Have you been following me? Stalking me?"

Edna wondered what Anita thought she was doing. She was purposely baiting him. Didn't she know her husband might snap at any moment and shoot them all? Her stomach in knots, Edna wished she could send some sort of signal to Anita to make her stop goading Rice. She looked around for something she could use as a weapon besides the tote bag she still held in her hands. If she struck him with something as harmless as a soft-sided bag, it might distract him enough to allow Yonny to overpower the older, less fit man, but it might also cause the gun to go off. Her eyes strayed to the window art hanging on a small suction cup as Rice answered his wife's accusation.

"I had to know where you were, who you were with." A slightly pleading whine had crept into his tone.

"You don't know what love is." Anita's voice was filled with contempt. "And the phone calls? What were all those calls for when you wouldn't say a word? I didn't think heavy breathing was your style, or were you waiting for a man to answer my phone?"

"What phone calls?"

Anita tossed her head with impatience. "You know what calls. The middle-of-the-night calls when you wouldn't speak. Those calls, as if you don't know." She crossed her arms over her chest and turned to look out the window past Edna's shoulder.

A look of amused tolerance crossed Rice's features. "So someone else has been after you. Probably one of your old boyfriends. Looks like I wasn't the only unfaithful one in this marriage, you hypocrite." He lifted the gun as if he were about to backhand Anita with it.

"Wait! Don't!" Edna shouted the words almost involuntarily as she took a step closer to the window. She had to keep Rice talking. She wasn't near enough to the circle of glass and metal yet. If only someone else would come along, someone who could help calm Rice down and get him to see that killing again wasn't the answer. He was looking at her, but he hadn't lowered the gun. Thinking frantically, she finally blurted, "Why kill Lia? Did she find out you were responsible for the Colliers' deaths?"

"What are you talking about? I didn't kill Lia." He frowned but lowered the gun to waist level as he looked at each of his hostages in turn, perhaps trying to determine if they all thought he had struck down Lia Martin.

Edna continued speaking her thoughts aloud, inching nearer to the window whenever Rice wasn't looking directly at her. "It seems too coincidental that Lia should be killed. She was not only a friend, but someone who could pass for Anita in looks and build." Something Grant had said returned to Edna. "Lia didn't usually run first thing in the morning. Anita was the one who ran mornings. Did you kill Lia mistaking her for your wife?"

"Go ahead." A small, high-pitched voice spoke from the doorway. "Tell her how much you wanted her dead."

Four sets of eyes turned to stare at Brea Tweed who seemed oblivious to the effect she was having on the others crowded into the small cabin. Steadying herself with a hand on the door, she brought one foot up to knee level and swatted at the dusty shoe with a tissue.

Twenty-One

"What are you doing here?"

Edna was relieved to notice that when Rice turned sideways to speak to Brea, he kept his eyes on Yonny. Apparently, he felt the other man was his worst threat, maybe his only threat. She sidled another half step closer to the window.

"Tell them," Brea repeated, lowering her foot, "that you promised to marry me as soon as *she*," Brea jerked her chin toward Anita, "was out of the way." Smiling, she sashayed over to Rice and put her arm through his, seemingly oblivious of the gun in his hand.

He took her wrist and, raising his gun arm momentarily, pulled her beneath his elbow and positioned her on his left side, his arm ending up around her shoulders. The move was accomplished as gracefully as a dance step. "What are you doing here?" he asked again. His eyes never left the hostages.

"Why, following you, Darlin'," Brea snuggled closer to him, putting one arm around his waist and looking up into his face. Then her smile turned to a pout. "I would have been here sooner, but I had to walk up the hill. Just look at my shoes."

Everyone in the room dropped their eyes to Brea's two-inch, sling-back heels. The black leather was coated with a fine layer of brown dust. Edna took a step closer to the window.

"Sweet Pea," Rice said. He tightened his grip so that his fist was beneath her chin and lifted her face so she looked up at him. "Forget your shoes. Why are you following me?"

"Rice, don't," Brea whined. "You're hurting me." She struggled to free herself, but Rice's grip was too tight. "I was on my way to Flatirons Crossing to do some shopping, and I saw you go by. You didn't even notice me. I wanted to see where you were going."

Rice was quiet for a moment, looking from Anita to Edna to Yonny, then back to Anita before glancing down at Brea. Edna held her breath and felt her fingers tighten on the tote she still held in front of her, but Rice didn't seem to notice her change in position. His eyes went around the room but didn't settle on anything. It was as if he was working something through in his mind. He relaxed his fist, putting his hand back on Brea's shoulder.

Anita had been staring at Brea. When she spoke, her voice shook with emotion. "You killed Lia?" Her words were both a question and an accusation.

Brea looked at Anita, her lower lip firmed in defiance. "It was an accident. I didn't mean to hurt Lia. I thought it was you."

Rice looked down at her in surprise but didn't seem alarmed. "What? Why did you want to do a thing like that?"

"I just told you." Brea pouted up at him. "I did it for you, for us. You said you'd marry me if you didn't already have a wife."

Rice let out a short laugh as if in disbelief. "I didn't tell you to kill her," he said.

"Not in so many words, but I knew you wanted her

out of the way. I figured I'd do it for you so you wouldn't have to. You know, sort of like a proxy." She seemed pleased she had come up with a sophisticated idea. When he didn't respond, she acknowledged the gun in his hand by nodding at it. "You're going to kill her now, aren't you?"

"Well, now, I guess that depends on how everyone behaves," he answered, but Edna knew by the hardness of his eyes that none of them would leave that house alive if Rice had his way. *He can't let any of us go, not even Brea,* she thought. *We all know too much, and Brea is a loose cannon.*

She was standing close enough to the stained glass circle now that she would be able to reach it easily, but she didn't want to make her move while Rice was pointing the gun. She needed a distraction.

"Go see if you can find something in the kitchen to tie them up with," Rice said to Brea, moving his hand to her back and giving her a shove. "Be quick."

As Brea stumbled through to the kitchen on the uneven wood floor, Rice waggled the gun at Anita, motioning her to move closer to Yonny who was now standing almost directly between Edna and Rice. Edna hadn't wanted to be blocked completely, since she had to watch Rice very closely. He pulled one of two straight-backed chairs from against the wall and placed it in the middle of the room. "Sit," he ordered Anita as he stepped back to grab the matching chair.

Instead of sitting, Anita put her arms out to Yonny, turning her face into his chest as he moved to her. Edna realized that they felt the same as she, that Rice wasn't going to let them live. Yonny put his arms around Rice's wife, pulling her against him and lowering his forehead to the top of her head. When Yonny moved, he blocked Edna's view of Rice but gave her full view of the front door and the window beside it. In that fleeting moment, she nearly gasped when she caught sight of Ernie's face disappearing beneath the sill.

Her heart began to pound. How long had he been outside? What was he up to? Was he going to come crashing through the door? She was about to grab for the glass circle when Brea came tottering into the room, her heels clicking on the floor boards. "Will this do?" She held what looked like a climber's rope in her hands.

"That'll do fine, Sweet Pea," Rice said, setting the second chair back to back with the first in the middle of the floor. "Bring it over here." Turning to Anita, he growled, "I told you to sit." He wagged the gun at Anita and Yonny. "Both of you. Over here."

Edna was frantic. She had to move soon. Where was Ernie? Why didn't he come through the door? What was he waiting for?

At the moment she decided she couldn't wait any longer, she heard a commotion in the direction of the kitchen and turned to see Greta come bounding into the room. Dropping her tote and grabbing the glass artwork, Edna stepped away from Yonny as she brought the disk across her body before flinging it out of her hand, aimed at Rice's chest.

Edna's motion must have caught his attention, because as the makeshift Frisbee came hurtling toward him, Rice bent backwards at his waist, dodging the missile. At the same moment, Greta jumped, her front paws landing in the middle of Brea's back. With a scream, she crashed into the chairs, falling in their midst, face forward to the floor.

Yonny, seizing the opportunity, leaped at Rice and spun him around while the older man was still off balance. The stronger rock climber threw his right shoulder against Rice's upper body, grabbing the gun arm at the wrist with both hands and forcing the barrel down towards the floor.

Greta, seeing her master struggling with a stranger, clambered over Brea's back and dove into the two men, knocking them backwards. Rice landed half on top of Yonny, but by that time, Greta had his wrist in her mouth. He dropped the gun with a howl. Entering from the kitchen, Ernie lumbered across the room and stooped to pick it up.

Twenty-Two

By the time the struggling stopped, the wail of sirens could be heard, and soon the tiny house was packed with uniformed police, both men and women. Escorted by one of the officers and followed by Greta, Yonny went into the back yard to give his statement. Edna and Anita were asked to step out front where each of them was seated in a different patrol car to be questioned. The whirling lights were finally extinguished, and curious neighbors were asked to return to their homes, where they pushed aside curtains or stood in their gardens to watch the show.

Ernie remained inside with the police and later reported to Edna that Brea kept demanding to be released because she had never meant to hurt Lia. She'd thought the woman was Anita, and besides that, she'd only done it because Rice practically told her to.

Rice Ryan remained mute and stony-faced, but if looks could kill, Brea would have been dead on the spot. Both Brea and Rice were cuffed and stored in separate vehicles to be transported to the Boulder County jail.

As the crowd in the tiny house diminished, Yonny came back inside to join Edna and Anita, who had given up their seats in the patrol cars to Brea and Rice. Ernie used the house phone to contact Paul Hartley, Mrs. Maitland's lawyer and Ernie's client, to give him the good news.

Although not willing to press charges against Yonny,

neither did Anita want to spend any more time in his company. She accepted Edna's offer of a ride back to Denver, and they set off, following Ernie's car back to the city. As they began the slow drive out of the canyon, Edna was surprised to see by the car clock that it was only two in the afternoon. It seemed to her that the entire day must have gone by, as exhausted as she felt.

"Mr. Hartley says he's arranged for a private jet to fly me to Rochester whenever I can get to the Rocky Mountain Airport." Anita had just finished talking on her cell phone, finalizing plans to visit her great-aunt, whose health seemed to be improving slightly, according to the lawyer. "Finding out I have a relative is still sort of hard for me to believe," she confided as she dropped the phone into a canvas tote at her feet.

"Speaking of relatives," Edna said, "would you like to go to the hospital and see Grant and his family before you fly off to New York?"

"I'd love it." Anita's response lit up her face. "I don't think another hour's delay will make any difference to my travel plans, and I've missed Jillian and Grant and Karissa so much. I wanted to call them a few times, but Yonny convinced me that the call would be traced. He had me so scared I didn't leave that house for the first two weeks I was there. He usually left me alone during the day, so Greta was a welcome companion. I think without her around, I would have gone crazy."

"They'll all be delighted to see you. They've been worried. We all have," Edna added emphatically.

"What has been going on while I've been secluded?" Before Edna could answer Anita added with tears in her voice, "I was so sorry to hear about Lia. Yonny didn't tell me she'd been killed until two days after her funeral. Can you believe that jerk? He knew she was my best friend."

"He probably knew that you would insist on attending her funeral. He couldn't risk it."

"He did treat me well. I have to admit that. He was always a gentleman and never once tried to hit on me. I felt so comfortable with him, so safe. How could I have been such a fool?"

"How were you to know? I thought he was very charming and sincere, too." Edna's words were followed by a brief silence while she concentrated on merging south onto Wadsworth Boulevard. Anita stared out the passenger-side window at the foothills.

Once she had settled more comfortably into the traffic pattern, Edna spoke again, telling Anita all she had learned and the worries they'd had over Anita's disappearance. Edna explained that if it hadn't been for Ernie's persistence, Anita probably wouldn't have been found before her great-aunt was gone.

"I hope to get a chance to talk with him at length, but that won't be until after I've been to Rochester. Maybe there's something I could do to show how much I appreciate what he did."

Edna slid her eyes toward Anita for an instant. "If you'd like my opinion, I have a feeling he'll need help with his wife's medical bills."

"Thanks for the tip. I'll definitely see what can be done."

As they approached the intersection at 92nd, the light turned red, and Edna could turn to speak directly to Anita without dividing her attention between driving and conversation. She nervously cleared her throat. "There's something else I'd like to ask of you, if I may."

"Anything." The young woman's face lit up. "Just name it."

"I'd like you not to mention my part in your rescue to Grant. Not right away, at any rate. Perhaps you could wait until you get back from visiting your great-aunt to give him the whole story. I should be home in Rhode Island by that time, and he'll be busy with the baby and other matters. He probably won't feel the need to scold me by then." She looked sheepishly at Anita. "And maybe he won't feel the need to speak to his father about my adventures. Albert worries about me, you know, and there's really no need. No need at all."

Anita's surprised expression turned to amusement, and a second or two later a giggle erupted from her throat, followed by another and another. Soon the two women were laughing heartily. A horn sounded behind them, letting them know the light had turned to green, and Edna drove forward, still chuckling.

"Mum's the word, if you'll pardon the expression," Anita finally managed to say before bursting into another fit of giggles.

When they arrived at the hospital, Edna left Anita at the front entrance, told her the room number, and went to park the car. They had agreed the young woman would go in ahead of her and give only the briefest explanation for her long absence. Anita would stay for a short visit, then call for a taxi to drive her home. Her own car had been left in her garage at the townhouse, and she would take that to the airport. She admitted to feeling a new sense of freedom and control and was anxious to drive herself instead of relying on anyone else for transportation.

Cruising the lot for a parking space, Edna spotted Ernie's car. She knew he'd been anxious about his wife. She would give him some time to check on Maxine and stop by the room later.

By the time Edna reached Karissa's room, Anita was sitting in a chair beside the bed, holding the baby and cooing to him. Jillian was standing beside her, one hand on Anita's shoulder, bending forward to give instructions on how to hold the baby so his head would be supported. Grant, sitting in a chair on the opposite side of the bed, was holding his wife's hand as they both beamed at their newborn son.

Karissa was the first to notice Edna. "Hello," she called, her face glowing with pleasure. "Look who finally showed up."

Of course, Edna and Anita had to pretend they didn't know each other. Per their arrangement, Anita had answered questions and told a condensed version of her story, leaving Edna out of it and involving only Ernie as her savior. Ernie would be instructed to do the same when Edna met him later in Maxine's room.

So Grant made introductions and Anita rose from her chair. "I'm sure this little guy would love to be with his grandmother," she said with a twinkle in her eye and a twitch to her lips. Edna could tell she was choking back laughter and tried not to show her own amusement.

Cradling the baby in her arms, she looked at Karissa and Grant. "Have you decided on a name for my newest little grandson?"

Before either parent could answer, a jangling note sounded from the cell phone on the bedside table. Grant picked it up quickly and answered without looking at the caller ID. After a second's pause he glanced at Edna, who was handing the now-fussing baby back to his mother.

"Oh, hi, Dad." Another brief pause before, "She's right here with us. No, I don't know why she wasn't answering her phone. Maybe it needs recharging."

Pause.

"Yes. Yes. Everyone's fine."

Pause

He watched Edna's face as he said, "Karissa wanted to name him after Mom."

Pause.

Laughing, he said, "Of course we didn't name him Edna. "We rearranged the letters of her name and came up with Dean. Dean Davies has a nice ring to it, don't you think?"

Apparently pleased with the reaction he'd seen on his mother's face, Grant turned and walked to the window where he stood looking out. He probably didn't want to disturb the rest of the group with his talking, but the acoustics in the room were such that his words could be heard plainly.

"Sure. We'll get her a ticket back to Rhode Island any time she'd like. We'd love her to stay for as long as she wants, but I know you miss her, and she must be anxious get home." Another pause.

"Yes, she does seem to spend a lot of time at the grocery store, Dad, but you know how Mom is. She's not happy sitting around all day with nothing to do. I'm sure she's been bored to tears."

Edna saw Anita glance over at her, and raising an eyebrow, she winked.

Meet Author Suzanne Young

Born and raised in New England, Suzanne Young has worked as a writer, an editor and a computer programmer since earning her degree in English from the University of Rhode Island in Kingston.

A resident of Colorado for almost 40 years, she recently retired from software development to write fiction full time. She is a member of Denver Woman's Press Club, Rocky Mountain Fiction Writers and Sisters in Crime, as well as a graduate of the Arvada (CO) Citizens Police Academy.

She welcomes you to visit her website at www.SuzanneYoungBooks.com and to write to her at Suzanne@SuzanneYoungBooks.com.

CPSIA information can be obtained at www.ICGtesting.com
265657BV00001B/16/P